I0706339

Cozy Up
to Blood

a novel about an island,
a cat, knitting, and vampires

by Colin Conway

Cozy Up to Blood

Cover design by Zach McCain

First Edition – 2020, Second Edition – 2023

ISBN: 978-1-961030-13-8

Original Ink Press,
 an imprint of High Speed Creative, LLC
1521 N. Argonne Road, #C-205
Spokane Valley, WA 99212

For Emsterraciousmikneek

Everybody be cool.

Seth Gecko (played by George Clooney)/
From Dusk Till Dawn

Chapter 1

The little white car repeatedly jerked with stops and starts into the parking lot of Forge's Gas and Auto Repair. Its wiper blades frantically flicked the rain away from the windshield. When the automobile came to its final resting place, Murray Lee slowly moved the gearshift into Park then turned off the engine. The Toyota Tercel didn't immediately stop, though. Instead, it sputtered a couple of times before loudly backfiring.

When the car eventually fell silent, the wiper blades stopped mid-stroke as if thankful they no longer had to fight a losing battle against a torrential downpour. Water cascaded down the cracked windshield. Untold thousands of droplets slammed onto the roof, creating a metallic symphony inside the car. The sun hid behind charcoal-colored clouds, and soon night would cover this part of the world.

Exhausted, Murray leaned forward to rest his head against the tilted steering wheel. The car's horn beeped a wimpy alert. The noise surprised him and caused him to bolt upright before wearily flopping backward into his seat. He looked toward the repair shop.

From inside, a bearded man in a stocking cap sipped from a large coffee mug and watched him with intense curiosity. Neither man made a move toward the other, as the rain provided a convenient excuse for the delay of immediate action.

A heavy pour had fallen in this part of the Pacific Northwest for more than two days now. The forecast predicted the hard rain was likely to continue for a few days longer before it turned into little more than a drizzle.

Across the street was the Golden Circle Grocer. On the side of the building, underneath a canopy, was a hand-painted mural that read *Welcome to Belfry*.

Before exiting the car, Murray put on a green John Deere baseball cap and flipped up the collar of his lightweight nylon jacket. Earlier in the day, he'd purchased both garments at a rural gas station. He popped open his door, which squeaked loudly, and he slipped into the pouring shower. He hunched his shoulders for additional protection from the rain while he hurried to the nearby structure.

Murray leaped over a large puddle on his way to the building. When he stepped inside, he was greeted not only with a pleasant *bing-bong* sound that announced his arrival but a warm blast of air.

The man with the salt and pepper beard sat on a stool behind the counter. He wore faded overalls and a red, long-sleeved T-shirt. From underneath a brown beanie, wavy gray hair fell to his shoulders. He removed an unlit match from the corner of his mouth. "Wet enough for you?"

It most assuredly was wet enough for Murray. It was also cold enough, windy enough, stressful enough, and late enough. However, he didn't feel like commenting on any of these, so he only frowned in response.

The clerk stuck the match back into his mouth, slid off his stool, and moved to the counter. He placed both hands into his pockets and was about to ask another question when he seemed to notice how big Murray was. The clerk was almost a head shorter than him. "Jeepers, you're a big fella."

The clerk's eyes took him in then. Murray knew the man was checking out the tightly rolled brim of his baseball hat, his nylon jacket, and finally, the inky ball of fire tattooed on his right hand.

"I take it you're not here for the festival."

"My car," Murray said, thumbing toward the lot. "It's—"

A three-legged pit bull hopped from around the corner of the counter. It was missing the front left leg. The dog's mouth hung open in either a toothy smile or a silent warning—Murray couldn't determine which.

"He won't hurt you none," the clerk said. "That's Wrecker."

At the sound of its name, the dog wagged its nubby tail. When Murray reached down to pet the animal, Wrecker pushed its head into his hand.

"He's a good judge of character. If he likes you, then I'll do the same." The clerk stuck out his hand. "Waylon Forge."

"Murray Lee." He shook the man's dirty, calloused hand. "You own the place?"

Waylon smiled. "That I do."

On a shelf behind the counter sat an old police scanner that squawked to life. *"Hey, Chief?"*

"Yeah, Colton? Gimme some good news."

Both Waylon and Murray turned their attention to the dusty black box.

"The State says the bridge is gonna be out for at least forty-eight hours, maybe seventy-two, unless there's a bigger break in the weather."

The radio screeched before the chief responded. *"What part of good news did you not understand?"*

Waylon smirked. "The local cops are decent fellas if a bit jittery. Know what I mean?"

"Jittery, how?"

"They tend to get into a man's business when they get nervous."

"They get into yours?" Murray asked.

The shop owner shook his head. "I got nothing for them to be nervous over."

"Hey, Chief, there's also a bunch of bikers lined up on the mainland."

Even though an unknown distance separated them, Waylon and the chief simultaneously asked the same one-word question. "Bikers?"

"You know," Colton replied. *"Some kind of motorcycle gang."*

"In this rain?" the chief asked. *"What are those idiots thinking?"*

"Whatever they're doing, they don't look none too happy."

"What do you think they want?" the chief asked.

"To cross the bridge," Waylon muttered. "Think, Chief."

Murray lifted a curious eyebrow, and the shop owner shrugged.

"There ain't much to do around here 'cept talk back to the radio."

The scanner squawked again. *"I guess they wanna cross the bridge,"* Colton said, *"but that isn't going to happen. At least, not today."*

"Keep an eye on them. See what they do."

Murray bent to scratch Wrecker behind the ear, and Waylon leaned over the counter to watch their interaction.

"You musta made it over 'fore the old bridge washed out," Waylon said.

"Barely," Murray muttered as he straightened. "That cop blocked it off just after I made the island. Then the water came over the top, making it impassable for anyone else."

"Uh-huh." Waylon gnawed on the match for a moment before saying, "Was a mistake coming onto the island."

"How's that?"

"We only got two bridges." The shop owner pulled the match from his mouth and pointed to the opposite end of town. "The new one's been under construction since spring. Shoulda been done by now, but it ain't and won't be for another month or so. So, with the old bridge washed out, we're all gonna be stuck on the island until the rain settles down and the water drops low enough for it to open again."

"Has it happened before?"

"The old bridge washing out? Usually about this time, but ain't nobody been worried about it this year since we all thought the other woulda been finished by now. So much for municipal efficiencies."

"There's no other way on or off?"

Waylon shrugged. "By boat, I guess, but you'd hafta leave your car. We ain't got no ferry."

Murray looked toward the parking lot.

"And probably not smart to go by water until the rain stops. Water's got to be choppy as all get out. The Columbia can be an unforgiving lady. She'll just as soon sink you as let you pass over."

Murray muttered, "Figures."

"So, what's the deal with your ride?"

He turned back to the shop owner. "She started doing the herky-jerk before I crossed the bridge. Didn't think I was going to make it across."

Waylon stuck the match back in his mouth. "What do you guess it is?"

"Oxygen sensor, maybe. Could be a fuel pump."

"You want I should take a look at it?"

Murray raised his eyebrows. "This *is* a repair shop, right?"

The shop owner's gaze floated toward a clock on the wall. It was almost five. "I'll check her out first thing in the morning."

"Any chance you'll stay late?"

"Nope. Gotta get home to the wife. They're voting on *Dancing with the Stars* tonight."

Murray stared at Waylon.

"Son, eyeballing me ain't gonna get me to stay. Besides, if I did get your car running, all you can do is drive around in a circle. You ain't getting off the island with the bridges bein' the way they are."

"Sounds like I don't have much choice in this matter." Murray tossed his car keys on the counter.

Waylon grabbed a clipboard and stuck a piece of paper under the clapper. "What's the license plate number of your car?"

"I don't know."

The shop owner looked outside. "It's raining too much for either of us to worry about it now. I'll get it later. Don't you worry none. Just sign here, and I'll get started on it in the morning."

Murray grabbed the pen but hesitated to sign.

"What's wrong?" Waylon asked with a playful snicker. "Forget your name?"

"Almost," Murray muttered. He then scrawled his signature across the bottom of the paper.

"Colton," the scanner crackled again.

"Yeah, Chief?"

"Get out to Abner Dewey's place," the chief ordered.

"I thought you wanted me to keep an eye on—"

Waylon clucked his tongue against the roof of his mouth but didn't comment. Instead, he took the pen from Murray and continued to fill out his form.

"Did he say someone bit a man?" Murray asked.

"Yup," Waylon said. "It's festival time, so all sorts of crazy things are likely to happen."

"What festival?"

Waylon looked up from the paperwork. "Haven't you heard of Belfry Island before?"

"No."

The shop owner tapped the pen against his chin. "Some years back, they made a few vampire movies here. All the girls, 'specially the teenaged ones, went crazy for 'em. Some of the boys, too. Now, every year them loonies come back to celebrate."

"What movies?"

"What's wrong with you, boy? Have you been living under a rock or something? They were only the biggest thing ever. Even I know about them and I ain't seen the darn things. You musta heard of *Evenfall*."

Murray shook his head. "I've been a little busy."

"That movie and its sequels made like a bajillion dollars. They were all the rage for some time."

A police car raced by the auto repair shop with its lights and sirens activated. Both men watched it pass.

Waylon removed the match from his mouth and licked his lips. "The fans of those movies come 'round every year. Occasionally, one of them does something foolish like trying to bite someone. Gotta be what happened out there at Abner Dewey's place."

"Weird."

"What can you do? People are strange."

"So, I'm stuck here for the night?" Murray said.

Waylon nodded. "At least. I don't keep a lot of parts on inventory. I may have to send over to the mainland if we need something and with the bridge being out..."

"I'm stuck," Murray dejectedly muttered.

"From the looks of it."

"Where do you recommend I stay?"

Waylon inhaled as he thought. "Normally, I'd say the Belfry Boarding House 'cause it's cute as a bug, but it's probably all booked up."

"The festival?"

"We only have a couple hotels on the island. A few folks will rent their houses out during this week. I can't wrap my head around that idea. Some of our visitors will stay on the mainland over in Astoria. That's where they made *The Goonies* back in the eighties. Ever see that one?"

Murray shook his head.

"Don't dig the movies, huh? Too bad. I liked it when I was a kid. Probably watched it half a dozen times on VHS. 'Hey, you guys!'" Waylon watched Murray for a reaction. When there wasn't one, he shrugged. "That was a line from one of the characters, but you wouldn't know about it, so I don't know why I just did that. Guess it's still one of my favorites. Astoria doesn't have a festival like we do, which is too bad because *Goonies* was a way better movie than any of the ones made here."

"I thought you said you didn't see the vampire flicks."

Waylon chuckled and looked slightly embarrassed. "Quit paying so much attention to what I say. You're making me nervous. Anyway, maybe someone didn't make it across the bridge, and you can get their room."

The shop owner stepped away from the counter, picked up a grease-covered phone, and punched several buttons. Waylon sipped from a large coffee mug while he waited for his call to be answered.

When it was, he had a quick conversation that Murray mostly ignored. Instead, he petted Wrecker, who seemed to be quite accustomed to spending time with visitors to the repair shop.

Waylon hung up the phone and grunted in satisfaction. "Like I figured. Someone didn't make it over, so they got a room available at the boarding house. They're holding it for you."

When the shop owner returned to the counter, he reached under it and pulled out a compact yellow umbrella. "I'll loan this to you until your car's done. You're gonna need it. We don't get much sunshine in this part of the world. This time of year, our skies are like standing under a weak shower head."

Murray reluctantly grabbed the umbrella and nodded his thanks. "Which way is the hotel?"

Waylon pointed up the street. "Head that way until you get downtown. You can't miss it."

After petting Wrecker a final time, Murray stepped to the door. "I'll come by tomorrow morning and check on the progress."

"Unless the vampires get you first," Waylon chuckled.

Murray's brow furrowed. "What?"

"I'm kidding. They're mostly harmless."

Chapter 2

He didn't notice them at first because they looked almost normal. After a while, though, he saw them everywhere.

The first couple were at the edge of downtown. Two fashionably dressed men huddled together under an umbrella. They wore expensive-looking suits, and their short dark hair appeared recently cut.

The rain continued to fall, and puddles along the curbs reflected neon signs and streetlamps.

As Murray approached the two men, they affected an air of casual disdain. When he was near, they froze as if statues and only their eyes followed him. Glitter covered the left sides of their faces.

After he passed them, they snickered and talked in hushed tones. For a moment, he worried they were laughing at the umbrella he held. It was the first time he'd used one—let alone a yellow one—and he felt oddly foolish for doing so.

That feeling quickly faded, however, as Murray noticed more smartly dressed men and women standing under their own umbrellas. Most stood still with the slouched posture and tilted heads of the previous men. Others walked in slow, elongated strides with exaggerated hip thrusts and dipping shoulders.

Murray stopped in front of a bookstore—The Thirst of the Mind. He continued to watch these people, especially those who moved languidly. It was as if they were bit actors in a movie montage. The effect on Murray was disconcerting, especially with how tired he felt.

Without looking, he pushed open the front door of the bookstore and backed in. He closed his umbrella and shook off the water. When he turned, he bumped headfirst into the glittering face of a young man with leering red eyes.

The fact the man was made of cardboard quickly lessened his shock, but Murray was surprised, nonetheless. Unfortunately, the life-sized cutout swayed slowly to the side and eventually fell to the floor between two tables of books.

"Edmund!" a female voice cried.

A mid-sixties woman hurried from around the sales counter and rushed toward the fallen cardboard portrait. When she rescued the downed cutout, she glared up at Murray. "How dare you!"

"It was an accident."

"This is Edmund!" She cradled the cardboard man's head in her hands.

"I didn't see him."

"How could you not?" she asked as she stroked Edmund's flat features. "He's so beautiful."

She righted the life-sized poster and dusted him off. Her fingers danced along its edges as she examined Edmund for any dings or folds. His hair was in a permanent muss, and his suit was perfectly tailored, just like the men and women he'd passed outside. The glitter on the left side of his cardboard face shone brightly under the store's lights.

When the woman was satisfied with Edmund's safety, she faced Murray. Her concern now diminished; she flashed the smile of a professional bookstore owner. "I'm sorry for my outburst."

"Don't worry about it."

"It's my year to host Edmund," she proudly said.

"You're taking care of a cutout?"

The woman's face pinched. "It's an honor to host the leader of Clan MacCrain."

"Clan MacCrain?"

Her lips pursed as her eyes ran his length. After assessing Murray, she said, "You are obviously not here for the festival."

"No, I'm—"

A brown cat wandered out then to investigate the commotion. It hesitated for the briefest moment, then continued toward Murray, where it rubbed itself against his leg.

The woman's face relaxed. "Rohan seems to like you."

Murray knelt to pet the cat.

"Cats are a good judge of character."

"Waylon Forge said the same thing about his dog."

The woman clucked her tongue. "Dogs are stinky saliva factories. Cats are stately." Her eyes narrowed when she asked, "Are you a dog person?"

He shrugged. "I have a cat."

That seemed to satisfy her as her smile returned. She offered her hand. "I'm Shirley," she said. "Shirley Herrick."

He stood, took her hand, and said, "Murray Lee."

"Nice to meet you, Mr. Lee."

"You, too." Murray bent to pet the cat once more. "And you as well... Morbius."

"Excuse me?" Shirley said.

Murray looked up. "It's my name for the cat. Morbius is a comic book vampire. I used to read it as a kid. Since it's a vampire festival, I figured I'd name the cat after—"

Shirley's face purpled. "First of all, this is *not* a vampire festival. It's an *Evenfall* festival. We do not recognize other vampires."

Murray opened his mouth to interrupt, but Shirley pointed at him in an accusatory manner.

"Second," she continued, "his name is Rohan. I don't know where you get off renaming my cat. That is by far the rudest thing I've ever had a customer do."

As he stood, Murray said, "I apologize."

"You should. It's disrespectful. Unbelievably so."

"It's a custom where I come from."

"To rename a cat?" Shirley glanced around as if she'd just heard the most awful thing imaginable. "Where in the world would anyone think renaming a cat is a good idea?"

"Pleasant Valley," he said.

"It doesn't sound pleasant."

"It's in Maine."

Shirley's lip quivered. "As I said, it sounds like a place for all cat lovers to avoid."

He hadn't meant to annoy the woman, so he returned the conversation to the cat's proper name. "So, Rohan, is it?"

Her face immediately brightened. "It means keeper of the wolves."

"Wolves?"

Shirley nodded knowingly, then lifted her hand to the side of her mouth as if she were sharing a secret. "Werewolves. They're everywhere. Rohan keeps them at bay."

"Your cat keeps werewolves at bay?"

She waved at him and tittered. "Not my cat, silly. Rohan MacCrain. From the movies."

"Edmund and Rohan?"

"Of course," she said, looking at him like he was some kind of alien. "Surely, you remember their names from the films?"

He shook his head.

"Read the books, then?"

"No. I just heard about them when I arrived here."

"Have you been on the moon or something? They're only the greatest things ever."

"And the movies were made in Belfry?"

"That's right. They filmed them before I moved here. I would have loved to have been part of that—to see the magic happen. Although, maybe it wouldn't be as exciting now if I got to see them made."

"Like working at a sausage factory."

"Exactly," Shirley said and pointed at him, but this time her finger was full of playfulness, not accusation. "Exactly!" she repeated.

"You moved here *because* of the movies?"

"Oh my, yes. Most of us did."

"Most of you?"

"We call ourselves The Evenfallers. I'd say half the town's population moved here because we saw the beauty the movies revealed."

"About vampires and werewolves?"

"Oh," she snickered, "we don't *really* care about the werewolves. The ones who do tend to live in campers."

"They camp?"

"No, silly. They live in RVs and trailers. You know the types—weirdos with dogs. There's usually a lot of them cramped into small spaces." She made a face. "Ugh. Dog people."

Murray politely smiled.

"Aside from the werewolves," Shirley said as she stole a glance at the cardboard Edmund, "the movies were just lovely. Even better than the books, if I'm honest. And I promise you, if you haven't seen them yet, your life will forever change. If you don't believe in true love before seeing them, you definitely will after."

Murray believed in love, although it was a rather new belief for him.

Shirley stole another glance at Edmund.

"What's with the glitter?" Murray asked. "I saw people wearing it outside."

Her eyes widened with excitement. "A vampire's skin shimmers when they walk in the sunlight."

"What?" Murray shook his head. "Vampires can't go in the sun."

Shirley rolled her eyes. "That's a silly, old vampire myth."

"No, it's not. That's vampire one-oh-one. Sunlight kills vampires."

The bookseller smirked. "You're wrong. Vampires can so go into the sun. There's hardly anything that can hurt them." Her eyes shimmered, and she was almost breathless in the manner some religious zealots speak.

Murray stared at her.

"They're God's perfect creatures," Shirley said, and she repeatedly nodded her head.

"They're the undead."

Her head stopped bobbing, and she set her jaw. "They've been given the gift of immortality. They're not the undead," she said with a sneer.

"They eat humans."

With a waggle of her finger, Shirley said, "Not this clan." She reminded him of a scolding teacher. "The MacCrains are vegetarians."

"Vegetarian vampires?"

She closed her eyes and nodded her head once in a definitive manner. "They eat animals. Not humans."

"That's not a vegetarian. That's still eating meat."

Her eyes popped open. "They control their thirst by eating animals."

"But it's not vegetarian," Murray said.

Shirley flexed her jaw a couple of times before saying, "You don't know what you're talking about. The MacCrains love us."

"They love... us?"

Shirley threw her hands in the air. "You don't understand anything. I don't know why I'm trying to explain this to you. You need to see the movies. They'll make you a believer."

Outside, a police car drove by with its lights blinking and its sirens blaring. When it passed, Murray turned back to Shirley, who now watched him with curiosity. Her hands were on her hips, and she leaned forward in a slightly challenging way.

"Is there something I can help you find, or did you just come in here to argue about the movies?"

He had entered the store mostly out of curiosity. Recently, he ran his own bookstore. But since he was here, he might as well take advantage of the opportunity. "How about a Travis McGee novel? *The Deep Blue Good-by.* John D. MacDonald wrote it."

Her face flattened.

"You haven't heard it of it?"

"Of course, I've heard of it." Her tone had turned frosty.

"Then what's the problem?"

"Mysteries." She almost spat out the word.

"What's wrong with them? Don't you carry those kinds of books?"

"Sure," she said. "I carry them. I've got to carry that kind of stuff for the normals. I wish our economy were different, but it is what it is." She turned and wandered deeper into the bookstore. "I think I've got a couple of his," she grumbled.

On the bottom shelf of the furthest wall were several John D. MacDonald novels. She bent over and slid out a paperback. "Here you go."

As she handed the book to him, he noticed a small tattoo on the inside of her wrist. Perhaps it was a hieroglyphic or text in another language, but she moved so quickly he couldn't make it out.

He turned his attention to the paperback novel. It was an old, dog-eared copy of MacDonald's first McGee novel. He had recently started reading another copy of the book. Unfortunately, he never got to finish it. He wanted to know how the story ended so he could talk about it with a particular reader he had met back east.

"I've got the second one in the series," Shirley said, "in case you want that, too."

Murray gently waved the paperback. "This will do for now."

As they walked back toward the counter, Shirley asked, "If you're not into the movies, what brought you onto the island?"

"Wrong turn," Murray said.

"That's unfortunate, especially with both bridges being out."

"I've been told."

"You'll probably be stuck here for a couple of days." The thought caused Shirley's face to brighten again. "You'll be able to join our festival and find out why so many of us love the story. On Saturday, we have a movie marathon at the theater where we show all three movies back-to-back. We also have celebrity signings, tours, a bonfire—"

"A bonfire?"

"Oh, yes. We reenact the big bonfire scene from the second movie. It's quite lovely and something to see. That's tomorrow night. You should come."

"I'll think about it." He held up *The Deep Blue Good-by*. "I need to pay for this."

Shirley stepped behind the counter and announced the price. Murray pulled a couple of bills from his pocket and handed them to her.

As she began the transaction, the front door opened, and a uniformed police officer stepped in.

Shirley saw him and said, "Evening, Colton."

"Hey, Shirley." The officer eyed Murray as he said, "Someone bit Abner Dewey out on his farm."

She stopped working the register and said, "Someone bit him? Is he okay?"

"The medics are with him now. Whoever did it pinched him pretty good. Even made him bleed."

Shirley glanced at Murray, then went back to the officer.

"We're pretty sure they wore fake teeth," Colton said. "The plastic kind." He shook his head. "Same kind most of our visitors wear this week."

"You're not suggesting it's an *Evenfall* fan, are you?" Shirley asked.

"You think a local would do that to Abner?" the officer asked.

The bookseller's eyes briefly lowered. "I guess not, but I hate to think that a fan of the movies—"

"It takes all types, Shirley," Colton said. "Abner described his attacker as big."

"Just big?" the store owner asked.

Colton's and Murray's eyes met. Murray stood several inches over six feet and weighed two-hundred-twenty-five pounds.

"Seen anybody that matches that description?" Colton asked, his eyes still on Murray's.

"Big?" Shirley said. "The only person who's been in recently is... I'm sorry I've forgotten your name."

Colton moved deeper into the store as his gaze traveled up and down Murray's frame. Uncomfortable with the officer's sudden attention, Murray nodded politely at the approaching man.

"I'd say you're about the size of Abner's attacker," Colton said.

"And what size is that?"

"About your size."

"That's pretty specific," Murray said.

The cop's eyes narrowed. "Where are you staying?"

"I don't have a room yet," Murray lied.

"You don't?" Colton leaned into Murray as his eyes carefully examined every inch of his head and neck area.

Murray said, "I wasn't planning on staying. My car broke down as I was passing through."

The cop stepped back. "Where's your car?"

"At Forge's. I dropped it there when I got into town."

"When was that?"

Murray wanted to tell another lie and say he'd been in town less than he had been. It was a natural response with a law enforcement officer. But he was with Waylon Forge when the report of Abner Dewey came in, so he had a perfect alibi. "I got into town about thirty minutes ago. Maybe forty."

The cop clicked his teeth together. "Shortly after the attack on Abner Dewey."

"Waylon and I heard about it on his scanner."

"You could have attacked Abner and driven over to Forge's to drop off your car as a way to establish an alibi."

"Why would I do that?"

"To establish an alibi," Colton said with a smirk. "I just told you."

"I mean, why would I bite this man, Abner? I don't know him. I don't know where he lives, and I've never seen the movies."

"It's true," Shirley said. "He didn't even know who Edmund was."

Colton pursed his lips, then moved them back and forth as he thought. "Whoever bit Abner also robbed him."

Shirley gasped then. The biting hadn't offended her sensibilities, but the robbery had. "Who would steal from Abner?"

"A biter," Colton mumbled as he leaned into Murray. "Maybe you stole from the old man and put the goods in the car that's sitting down at Forge's. That seems like a good plan on how to hide something you stole."

"That's a plan," Murray agreed. "Not a good one, but it's a plan."

"That's what I was thinking," the officer said, as he noticed the fireball tattoo on the back of Murray's hand. "What did you say your name was?"

"I didn't."

Colton cocked his head.

"Murray," he said flatly.

The officer's eyes narrowed. "Your first name only, huh? Cute. Why do I get the feeling you've had police contact before?"

"Murray Lee."

Colton snapped his fingers. "Lemme see your ID."

Murray doubted he needed to show his driver's license, but he decided not to fight the officer's power play. Being stuck on an island for a few days with an irate cop was not an ideal way to spend his time. Being nice seemed the right move. He dug out his wallet, removed his driver's license, and handed it to the cop.

Colton copied the pertinent information into his notebook before handing it back to Murray.

The officer's eyes traveled a final time up and down Murray's length. "All right, Mr. Lee. I'll talk with Waylon and see if your story checks out. You better hope it does."

"He's closed now," Murray said.

Colton's eyes narrowed.

"*Dancing with the Stars* is on tonight," he explained.

"You got an answer for everything, huh?"

"Not everything."

The officer sucked something imaginary through his teeth. "The morning then. Don't go anywhere before we can have another talk."

"Where am I going to go? The bridges are out."

For the first time, Colton smiled.

After the officer left, Shirley said, "Don't worry about him none. There's never any real excitement here in Belfry. Whenever something even remotely interesting happens, ol' Colton just has to swing into action."

"Like Batman?"

"No, silly. Like Rohan."

Shirley handed Murray his book and change. As he headed for the door, she called after him, "Stay safe out there. You don't have Edmund or Rohan to protect you."

Chapter 3

Three days ago, with members of the Satan's Dawgs Motorcycle Club chasing him, a man formerly known as Owen Hunter fled the colorful city of Costa Buena, California.

A couple of weeks before that, a man identified as Brody Steele raced away from the east coast town of Pleasant Valley, Maine. He also had members of the Satan's Dawgs nipping at his heels.

In reality, the Dawgs weren't interested in either Owen or Brody. Instead, they wanted the man who lived under both those pseudonyms.

Beauregard Smith, the former bookkeeper for the Dawgs, had recently turned informant and slipped into the U.S. Marshal's Witness Protection Program.

Before fleeing his last cover identity in Costa Buena, U.S. Marshal Theodore 'Ted' Onderdonk handed Beau, aka Owen Hunter, an envelope containing a new identity and a thousand dollars in cash. Together with FBI Agent Max Ekleberry, Onderdonk had stayed behind to slow down the members of the motorcycle club who discovered their witness hiding in California.

A handful of the Satan's Dawgs must have slipped by the lawmen, though, since they chased Beau north. For a time, he lost them in a long line of traffic caused by construction on U.S. 101.

His first stop after fleeing Costa Buena was the northern California town of Eureka. It took some time, but he eventually found a pay phone near the public library. He didn't have a cell phone. Carrying one, even the disposable ones called burners, made it too easy for someone to track him.

After dropping several coins into the phone, he placed a call to Ace Adventures, the front created by the Marshal Service to allow Beau a safe and secure way to contact Onderdonk. The call was answered after the first ring.

"Ace Adventures," a pleasant female voice said, "where your journey begins. How may I help you?"

He knew the marshals would trace the call to this location. Perhaps it wouldn't take very long to do so like it did in the movies. Maybe they would instantaneously know where he was. The thought did not bring him additional comfort.

He pressed the phone tightly to his ear. "Mr. Onderdonk, please."

"May I ask who is calling?" The woman's tone had turned cautious.

"This is..." he couldn't remember his new cover name. The little envelope was still in the white car parked around the corner. He rubbed his forehead and said, "Beauregard Smith."

He could hear her tapping on a keyboard a moment before two motorcycles roared past the library. Their attention was on the road, so they didn't see him standing in the phone booth.

"Perhaps your reservation is under a different name."

"That's my real name."

"Sir," the woman exasperatedly said, "you're not supposed to—"

"I know what I'm not supposed to do," Beau snapped. "I need to talk with Onderdonk. Can you get a message to him?"

"Mr. Onderdonk is—" She paused, as if considering her next word carefully. "—indisposed."

Two more motorcycles drove by the library. He imagined they would ride quickly through town, checking for his white Toyota, then get back on the 101 and hurry north.

Gripping the phone tighter, Beau asked, "The heck does that mean? *Indisposed?*"

"It means he's unavailable at this time. We'll send someone else to meet you."

He felt something he didn't often feel—worry. Ted Onderdonk wasn't a friend, but Beau had developed a sort of affinity for the marshal. It was the same way a drowning man develops a connection to a life preserver. "Did something happen to Ted?"

"Mr. Smith," the operator said, "I see you're in—"

"What about Ekleberry?"

"Excuse me?"

"Ekleberry," Beau repeated loudly.

"I heard you the first time," she said. "But yelling at me does not make it any clearer. What's an Ekleberry?"

"He's an FBI agent."

"Oh, well, I'm sorry. We don't track their people."

Beau's frustration rose. "Can't you work together in this situation? Maybe get him a message."

"Sir, please understand. We have rules you must follow."

"Tell me what happened to Onderdonk. He's my witness inspector. You owe me that much."

"Sir," the operator calmly said. "Stay where you are. We've got someone en route to you now. They'll be there in fifteen minutes. They'll tell you everything."

He dropped the telephone receiver as if it had burned him. He didn't want someone else to come for him. It felt odd to admit this, but he didn't want to trust anyone except Marshal Ted Onderdonk or Agent Max Ekleberry.

The telephone receiver swung gently from its cord as he stepped back from the phone. Right now, he had one choice.

Run.

With a final glance around the library, Beau bolted toward his car. His head swiveled left and right, continually searching for members of the Satan's Dawgs.

They had tracked him this far north, so it was time to adjust his plan.

***

He drove east until he came to Redding, where he refilled his gas tank. His new plan was to run east, but now he was second guessing that. Maybe he should head north again into Oregon, but he thought that's what everyone would expect him to do.

When he put the fuel nozzle away, he dropped into the driver's seat, returned to the freeway, and headed south. Driving deeper into California was an irrational plan, but he needed time to think.

Without Onderdonk or Ekleberry in his corner, he felt lost. Counting on two lawmen to help him was a new feeling.

It felt unnatural.

It felt wrong.

While with the Satan's Dawgs, he rarely needed anyone's help to do his job. As their bookkeeper, he often worked alone to dispense the club's distinct brand of justice.

To hide positions of authority, the club coded them in such a way as to disguise their true meaning in case anyone in law enforcement ever heard members of the club talking. Beau was the club's bookkeeper, which meant he "kept book" on those who crossed the Dawgs.

That could mean anything from stealing from the club, hijacking one of its shipments, or assaulting a member. Whenever an account entered Beau's book, he would soon clear it. He had taken great pride that his books were always in balance. A long line of injured and dead men proved that.

But now he needed the assistance of the law not only to keep him safe but to help keep him on the path of right. He wanted to live a different life, to be a better man. He wanted to do this not only for himself but for a woman he had met only weeks ago. Even though he worried they could never indeed be together, he still wanted to do it for her.

He drove through towns like Red Bluff, Chico, and Yuba City. Shortly after five in the afternoon, he finally stopped in Placerville. His hunger had reached a point where he could no longer ignore it.

For a moment, he considered driving through the northern California city and moving on. When he entered the quaint downtown, a sign announced: Welcome to Placerville - "Old Hangtown." Multiple businesses had versions of the city's nickname in their names—Hangman's Hardware, Hangtown Realty, and Hang in There Yoga. One antique store—Hang-Out in the Past— even hung a weathered noose from the front of their store. Beau figured it was all a marketing ploy built around the city's past, so he let it slide. It might be a bad omen, but his hunger was more significant than his trepidation.

There were several fast-food restaurants he could visit, but he wanted to sit somewhere children and families wouldn't be likely. He also wanted to go where there wouldn't be loud or boisterous crowds. Therefore, he ignored any place that had a sports atmosphere or pizza in its name.

He wandered into a little bistro and waited for a host. A mid-forties server with heavy make-up and a disapproving smirk approached to eye him with suspicion.

Beau wore a blue T-shirt that read *Rockafellers*, faded blue jeans, and Converse tennis shoes. The tattoos that ran the length of both his arms were visible.

"Table for one?" she asked in a slow and accusatory manner.

She placed him in the far back corner at a two-person table. When she pulled back his chair, the legs scratched across the concrete floor. The resulting screech caused several patrons to face him with annoyed looks. The server handed him a menu, announced the soup of the day—a roasted butternut squash—and hurried into the back.

Nearby, a couple of other servers pushed together two tables for an incoming group.

"Pay attention to these ladies," the older female server said.

The young male server nervously smiled. "What about them?"

"They may look sweet," she said, "but mess up their orders, and you'll pay for it."

"You want the table?" the young man asked, clearly concerned he was in over his head.

"Not a chance," the older server said and hurried away.

Beau opened his menu flat, placed his elbows on the table, and rested his head in his hands. It was then that weariness overtook him. He yawned, and the words on the paper menu blurred.

He heard the voices of many women enter the restaurant and proceed to the nearby tables. He didn't bother to look up as he felt himself drifting off.

"I heard the news was there and everything," a woman said.

"The man they were protesting was awful," another commented. "Just awful."

"The worst," yet another added. "He was not community-minded at all. A terrible man."

"Cro-Magnon," a fourth tossed out.

"What was his name again?"

"Hunter Owen or something like that."

"No," corrected another. "It was Owen. Owen Hunter."

Beau's eyes popped open, but he kept his face hidden in his hands.

"Owen," the first woman said. She repeated the name as if it tasted terrible. "Owen. Eww."

Another woman said, "I once knew an Owen. Dreadful man. Just dreadful. Smelled of Nilla Wafers and lived with his mother."

While in Costa Buena, Beau, aka Owen Hunter, had run afoul of several groups who banded together to protest the record store that he operated, which was really a U.S. Marshal front. It turned into an ugly scene that made national news and was plastered all over social media. It was the reason the Satan's Dawgs were able to find him.

Those most responsible for the proliferation of bad news were a band of older women called The Purple Hat Coalition. They had no plan except continued civil disobedience. They would glom onto any protest, regardless of its cause, and support it. With their help, the Purple Hat Coalition could push a rally further than it could go on its own.

As Owen Hunter, Beau had managed to offend the local leadership of The Purple Hats.

"That man," a woman with a high voice said, "said dogs were better than cats."

"He did not!" another exclaimed.

"He did! He most certainly did. It's on the YouTube."

"Helen, it's just YouTube. You don't have to say *the*."

"I don't understand," Helen said.

"It's just YouTube. The *the* is implied."

Beau removed his hands from his face and looked up from his menu. His stomach turned sour, and his mouth was dry.

He didn't turn to the ladies next to him, as he was afraid to make eye contact and bring attention to himself. He planned to stand and leave the restaurant quietly. Hopefully, the women would never know he was nearby.

As he stood, his chair scratched loudly across the concrete floor. The screech caused all eyes in the restaurant to turn his way.

"Oh my God," several women shouted. "It's him!"

When he faced them, Beau only succeeded in confirming his worse fears. Seated next to him were eight older women in various hats.

A couple wore berets. Another wore a Posie. There were two fedoras cocked at jaunty angles. One woman with platinum blond hair wore a Victorian top hat with a peacock's feather stuck in its band. The rest sported bell hats.

The head coverings shared a common element, though. They were all purple.

At the edge of the table stood a wire stand with a hand-printed placard. It read *Reserved for The Purple Hat Coalition of Placerville.*

The woman in the Victorian top hat stood, pointed a crooked finger, and ordered, "Get him, ladies!"

Several of the women pulled out their phones and photographed Beau.

"What are you doing?" he wearily asked. He was too tired to fight with a group of senior citizens.

The woman with the top hat announced loud enough for the whole restaurant to hear, "Owen Hunter, you are at the top of our most-wanted list."

He glanced around the establishment. Several patrons watched in fascination as some of the silver-haired women took his picture. Others in the group fiddled with their phones.

"What did I do?"

"A cat is not a dog," the leader of the coalition loudly pronounced.

Several of the women hissed as they typed on their phones. There was a murmur of support from the rest of the restaurant.

"I never said that," Beau whined. He actually did whine, and he cringed when he heard himself do so. It must have been the lack of sleep.

The leader of the group pointed again at him. "Yes, you did say that. Our Costa Buena chapter reported it."

"So what if I did?" he asked and threw up his arms in resignation. "What's with the pictures?"

Several of the women held up their phones and simultaneously said, "Done!"

The woman in the top hat smiled. "We've just alerted all our sister organizations that you are in Placerville. You will never be welcomed as long as we can find you."

Several of the restaurant patrons clapped while others held up their phones to take photos of Beau.

"You've got to be kidding me," he mumbled.

"We never kid, Mr. Hunter. We don't have the time for it."

He hung his head. Not only was he running from the Satan's Dawgs and the east coast mafia, now he'd have to be careful of little old ladies.

"We will hound you to the ends of the earth," the leader of the women announced. The peacock feather attached to her hat bounced as she moved excitedly about.

Beau lifted his head and immediately went for the exit. The last thing he heard as he made the sidewalk was the woman yelling from inside the restaurant, "You'll never be safe from us!"

Two tables of silver-haired women cheered in excitement.

Chapter 4

Inside the front door of the Belfry Pharmacy was another cardboard cutout. This one was of a shirtless young man in torn jean shorts. He was hunched slightly over with his shoulders flared wide. Tanned skin pulled taut across bulging chest muscles while his stomach rippled in a washboard fashion. His hands were splayed open and held away from his body. Bright white teeth were bared in what might have been a grimace but came surprisingly close to a smile. No shoes were on his bare feet.

"He's beautiful, isn't he?" a female voice said.

A woman in her early forties approached. She wore a pharmacist's smock, and her mousy brown hair was tucked behind her ears. A Belfry Pharmacy name tag was sewn onto her white coat and announced her name underneath, in cursive, as Pam Benson.

Once near, she caressed the cutout's shoulder and carefully examined it as if she'd never seen it before.

"Who is he?" Murray asked.

Pam turned to him as if offended.

"I've never seen the movies," he said.

Her offense turned to disdain.

"Is he homeless?"

"What?"

"He doesn't have a shirt, and he's barefoot."

Pam raised her eyebrows and spoke slowly, as if talking to a child. "He's a lycan."

"Is that the thing with the wheat allergy?"

Her mouth slowly dropped open.

Murray turned back to the cutout. "He seems too buff to be into only vegetables—unless he's juicing. Steroids, I mean."

The pharmacist frowned. "I know what you mean, and I can assure he's not taking steroids."

"Then why's he look like that?"

"The uninformed might call him a werewolf," Pam said flatly.

Murray frowned. "Huh."

"You're not impressed."

"Not really."

"Why not?"

"He's not scary. Is he supposed to be?"

Pam blinked several times. "He's not... That's all you can say? He's not scary. This magnificent man is Spartan, leader of the Moon Children."

Murray chuckled. "Moon Children."

Pam shoved her hands into the pockets of her smock. The action pulled the blue garment tight around her shoulders. "You're mocking it."

"No. I'm sorry. I'm not mocking it."

"Why are you in Belfry if you don't like the movies?"

"Wrong turn."

The pharmacist eyed him skeptically. "And now you're stuck because of the bridge?"

He nodded.

"So, you're a non-believer?"

"It's okay," he shrugged. "I don't believe in Star Wars, either."

Her lip curled. "That's science fiction."

"There's a difference?"

She clucked her tongue against the back of her teeth. "What do you want?"

"Aspirin and a cell phone. One of the prepaid jobs. Do you carry those?"

Pam led him down an aisle and pointed to the pain relievers. "The phones are behind the counter. We can never be too safe when mainlanders visit." The way she distastefully said "mainlanders," Murray knew she meant him. Pam disappeared around a corner while he selected a brand of headache reliever.

When he returned to the front, there were several prepaid cell phones laid on the counter. He selected each in turn and studied them. When he was with the Satan's Dawgs, he often carried one of these and threw them away whenever necessary.

Before this current situation, however, he wouldn't have considered buying one. Marshal Onderdonk had told him to avoid anything that could track him—social media, computers, and cell phones.

Skipping social media wasn't that big a deal as he never had an account on any of the services. Besides, he never found the idea of sharing pictures of himself alluring. Why would the world be interested in what he was doing? And he sure as heck didn't want to know what anyone else was doing, especially if they had kids or cats. Maybe a cat picture or two wouldn't be so bad, but he didn't want to see any baby pictures. People could keep those to themselves.

And he only used computers when necessary. He never had an email account, so that wasn't even a sacrifice. Murray's computer knowledge was about a step above knowing where the power button was. He wasn't proud of not understanding computers, but he was comfortable enough with himself to know his limitations.

But cell phones, those Murray understood as he had used many burners before. They were a tool of the trade—used and tossed with frequency. He threw away cell phones because they were traceable. Because of that, he handled them with ultimate care.

If he contacted someone that anyone else was observing, then they could backtrack that call to his burner phone. He knew it required sophisticated software—maybe even hardware—but today, software and hardware were not limited to government agencies.

Groups that wanted him dead were pursuing him, and they had both human resources and money. They even had a custom-made website. He imagined it would take a fair amount of skill to create one, so how much more ingenuity would be necessary to track down his cell phone?

Beyond the danger of being traced, Murray also knew a cell phone would tempt him to call a specific person in Pleasant Valley, Maine.

Calling her could put her at risk if anyone were to find out. He might already have put her at risk by sending her the occasional letter, but he wanted to let her know that he was thinking about her. And mail seemed less conspicuous in this current digital environment.

"I'll pass," he said and set the final cell phone box down.

"Just the aspirin?" Pam asked.

He hadn't had time to grab anything before fleeing Costa Buena. This was a perfect opportunity to pick up some additional sundries. "I also need a toothbrush and toothpaste."

"No problem," the pharmacist said.

"And a comb and some deodorant."

"We've got those, too."

She walked around the counter and headed toward an aisle. As she pointed to various items, he grabbed them indiscriminately—he didn't have brand loyalty.

"Anything else?" she said.

"What about a postcard? Got any of those?"

Pam returned to the counter and pointed to a nearby spinner.

As he searched through the postcards, Murray asked, "Did you hear about the attack at the Dewey property?"

"You know Abner?" Pam asked. She seemed surprised.

Murray shook his head as he flipped through the small cards. "I heard it on the police scanner when I was with Waylon Forge. The biting thing. That's interesting."

"Not really," Pam said. "It's happened before, although it's been a couple of years."

She fell silent and watched Murray peruse the postcards. Most of them had images with comments like *Belfry Island, Oregon—the Official Home of* Evenfall; *Take a Bite Out of Belfry; Howl at the Moon in Belfry;* or Murray's favorite, *Belfry Sucks,* which featured a photograph of Edmund with blood dripping from his mouth.

Pam rested an elbow on the counter and leaned her weight on it. "This wouldn't happen if Spartan was on the island."

Murray glanced toward the cardboard cutout at the front of the store. "What's that?"

"The biting of Abner Dewey. When lycans are around, there's peace between vampires and humans. None of them would think about attacking a human."

"I'm not following," Murray said.

"Lycans protect humans. They keep the vampires at bay."

Murray's brow furrowed. "Werewolves protect people?"

"*Lycans,*" Pam said. "*Lycans* protect humans."

"What's the difference between a werewolf and a lycan?"

The pharmacist sighed. "Werewolves only transform by the light of the moon. They're sort of stupid, but lycans can shapeshift at will. That's why I'm loyal to the Children of the Moon and what they stand for. They've banded together against the vampires to protect the island's inhabitants."

"But I thought they only ate animals. The vampires, I mean."

Pam shook her head. "That's what they *want* you to believe."

"They?"

"The vampires. They thirst for blood."

"I heard some of them only ate animals."

Pam rolled her eyes. "That's the MacCrains. All the other vampires eat humans. To them, we're just long pigs."

Murray rubbed his head. The whole concept of *Evenfall* was ridiculous. The story took place on a small island off the Oregon mainland in the Columbia River. Blood-thirsty vampires, some of which ate animals instead of humans, hung out there. Lycans protected humans rather than ravage them. The whole thing sounded rather—

"Silly," Pam said. "That's what you're thinking, I know, but until you see it or read it, you can't understand the beauty."

"Beauty?" he asked.

Pam's expression showed the same religious devotion that Shirley from the bookstore had. "Oh my God, yes."

"You know the movies aren't real."

"They're real enough for the fans who come to the festival. They're real enough for those of us who have moved here to live out our lives in the wonder and glory of Belfry."

Wonder and glory?

A seriousness returned to Pam's face. "Listen. I'm not crazy. I know they're only movies. But they came from lovely books birthed by the imagination of a heavenly-inspired woman."

Heavenly inspired?

"So what if we love them?" Pam asked. "Where's the harm in that?"

"Someone is biting other people," Murray said. "That sounds kinda harmful."

"Which was my original point. This would never have happened if there was a lycan around. If any of the festival attendees pretended to be one of them, things like this wouldn't occur. But, oh no, all anyone ever wants to be is a vampire dressed in their fancy clothes with their stupid, sparkly skin and pouty lips." Pam pushed out her lower lip.

"No one wants to dress in ripped jean shorts without a shirt and shoes?" Murray asked.

"No," Pam muttered.

"Probably because it's hard to get service at a restaurant."

"I know!" Pam tapped the counter. "That's what I've said at the Chamber of Commerce meetings, but most of the restaurant owners refuse to amend their rules for festival week."

"Maybe it's a health code thing."

"It's a vampire thing," she said with a smirk. "Vampires spend better."

"You mean fans of the vampires, right?"

"Stop splitting hairs. Regardless, it doesn't matter because no one comes dressed as a lycan."

"Maybe because it's cold and rainy this time of year."

Pam dismissively waved her hand. "That's not it."

"Which begs the question," Murray said, "why are you holding the festival in fall? Why not in the summer when kids could come?"

"*Evenfall* isn't for kids," Pam said with a derisive snort. "We don't want children around."

Murray smiled. Maybe *Evenfall* was a series he should check out. Anything promoted as a kid-free event was something he might enjoy.

"And the movies took place in the fall," Pam said. "We're trying to be true to them, which is why I think that's the problem with the lycans."

"What do you mean?"

"At the end of the series, the lycans left the island."

"Shirley from the bookstore said some fans of the lycans live nearby in RVs and trailers. She doesn't seem to like them very much."

"She was talking about my neighbors and me. She probably said something about my dogs, too. What else did she say?"

"Nothing."

Pam chuckled. "I doubt that. She's a familiar, and that should tell you all you need to know."

"A familiar?"

"People who pledge themselves to a vampire house. She's got a stupid tattoo—" Pam tapped the inside of her wrist. "—that shows she belongs to the MacCrains. Whatever. Like that means anything. The Moon Children don't require any stupid pledge."

Murray's brow furrowed.

"Anyway," the pharmacist continued, "since only the MacCrain clan remained on the island, that's why you have someone running around biting people. There's nothing to balance the scourge of the vampire."

"This whole thing—" Murray thumbed toward the cutout at the front of the store. "The vampires, the lycans, Belfry. It's hard to believe people are so into it."

She inhaled deeply and stared at him for a moment. Finally, she said, "You can believe what you want to believe."

"I'm sorry if I offended you."

Pam shrugged. "The movies revealed what we all know is true. It was time somebody showed it."

There was crazy, Murray thought, and then there was just plain weird. He'd only met a portion of the community, but he believed this whole town would fall firmly into the bizarre category. He pushed the various items he'd selected toward the pharmacist. "This will do."

She rang the items up, shaking her head as she did. "I know I sound like a broken record, but we need the balancing power of a lycan. Even one would do. They're the only thing that can protect us."

"What about the police?"

She barked a single laugh, paused her tapping on the register, then continued laughing at the idea of police helping with vampires.

Murray felt the same general way about the police, but he didn't join in her laughter. He didn't want to encourage the crazy or the weird.

Pam studied him. "You know... you're big enough to be one of them."

"One of what?"

"A lycan."

"I'm not, though."

"No," she said with a nervous giggle. "Of course not."

She looked away, then glanced at him, before muttering, "Besides..."

"Besides what?"

"You're too old."

"I'm not too old," he blurted. "I'm thirty-five."

"As I said," she muttered, her tone flat with disappointment. "Too old."

Chapter 5

At the Belfry Boarding House, another cutout met him near the lobby's entrance. This one was of a small woman. She wore a hooded sweatshirt, blue jeans, and red tennis shoes. Her face was permanently in an angry pout.

A young man with short, dark hair approached. His name tag read *Sebastian*. He wore black slacks, a white shirt, and a dark purple vest. The color combo matched the painted walls of the small hotel lobby.

A well-dressed man and woman entered the waiting room and watched Murray and Sebastian. They huddled together. The man's arm was wrapped tightly around the woman's waist while her head rested on his shoulder. Both were tall and wore what appeared to be tailored suits. His was blue, and hers maroon. On his wrist shone a gold watch that looked nicer against her outfit than his own.

She was extremely pale with glitter on the left side of her face and appeared to have the constipated look Murray now associated with the vampires. He, however, was tan and glitter-free.

"Checking in?" Sebastian asked.

"Yeah," Murray said, turning his attention back to the attendant. He jerked his head toward the cutout. "Who's that?"

Sebastian lifted his eyes to the ceiling. "Adela."

"You don't like the movies?"

The young man's lip curled. "They were atrocities. Complete disasters. Each one worse than its predecessor."

"But the festival—" Murray started.

"This cardboard caricature—" Sebastian flicked the cutout with a finger. "It could act better than the actress they hired. But what do I know? Beauty has her way, I guess. The girl ended up in a comic book movie after *Evenfall*. Now, she's like the highest-paid actress in Hollywood. Just ridiculous." His eyes scanned around Murray's legs. "No bags?"

"None."

Sebastian walked off toward the counter, and Murray followed. He watched the attendant's fingers dance across a computer keyboard.

"How do you know so much about the movies if you hate them?"

"I read," Sebastian said. "Do you have a reservation?"

"Waylon Forge called for me."

"You're Mr. Lee? Lucky for you, the bridge washed out."

"In more ways than one."

Sebastian glanced at him sideways, but Murray offered no further explanation.

"Driver's license and credit card," the attendant said.

"I don't have a credit card. Just cash."

"You'll have to pay in advance, then. I can give you two days. Maybe more if the bridge doesn't open up."

"Two days will be fine."

Murray laid his driver's license on the counter, along with several bills. "So, the books are better than the movies?"

Without looking his way, Sebastian said, "Isn't that always the case?"

"Sure," Murray said, although truth be told, he hadn't read a book since high school. He glanced down at the Travis McGee novel that he held in his hand. Murray realized he could now amend that statement—he hadn't *finished* a book since high school.

As Sebastian's fingers continued to click on the keyboard, he said, "The books touched me, especially the second one, *Crescent Ascent*. It's such a beautiful story."

"Huh."

Sebastian stopped typing and studied Murray. "I apologize. You probably loved the movies, and I've offended you."

Murray shrugged. "Not me. I've never read the books or seen the movies."

"Where have you been?" Sebastian asked. "In Siberia?"

Prison, Murray thought, *at least for part of the time.*

And there was no way the guys inside were going to watch romantic vampire flicks. The same went for the club. No one in the Dawgs ever read any books regardless of their content, and the movies they watched always had plenty of explosions, gun battles, or naked women.

"I must have missed them," Murray said.

"Crazy," Sebastian muttered and returned his attention to the computer. "What brought you to Belfry?"

"Wrong turn."

"Lucky for you."

"You already said that."

The door to the hotel opened, and a heavy-set man walked in. He wore a brown, hooded raincoat that shimmered with wetness. Water dripped onto the carpet.

Sebastian glanced toward the visitor but remained silent.

The man clomped over toward the desk, purposefully stomping with each step to remove excess rain from his boots. When he stood near Murray, he eyed him up and down. Next, he scrutinized the couple in the lobby.

They had moved to the love seat where they now canoodled. The heavy-set man grunted his disapproval, then turned his attention back to Murray.

He unzipped his raincoat and pushed it open by placing his hands on his thick leather belt. This move exposed a gun and a handcuff case. On his left breast was a shiny silver badge, while on his right was a blue name tag inscribed *Kern*.

With his attention still on the computer, Sebastian absently asked, "What can I do for you, Chief?"

"Hear about Abner Dewey?"

The attendant placed a piece of paper on the counter, held a pen, and told Murray, "Sign here." To the chief, Sebastian said, "What about Abner? What's he complaining about now?"

"He got himself bit, is what he did."

A snicker came from the couple on the couch.

The lawman's head whipped to them. "Think that's funny, Charlie?"

The couple broke their embrace. "Excuse me?" asked the man.

"You think that's funny? A local getting himself bit."

The man on the couch frowned. "We were enjoying a kiss, Chief. That's why we giggled."

The chief frowned. "People don't laugh when they kiss."

The woman pouted. "Oh, that's sad. You don't make someone happy when you kiss her?"

Kern's face reddened. "Watch it, girlie."

The couple giggled and returned to snuggling.

The chief watched them for a few seconds longer. The corner of his lip twitched several times. Finally, he turned back to the men at the counter. "Abner gave us a description of his attacker—"

"Abner's okay then?" Sebastian asked.

"Of course, Abner is okay," Kern said. "Why wouldn't he be okay?"

"Well," the attendant said, "if he got bit by a vampire, he'd be dead, right?"

"Or he'd turn into a vampire," Murray offered.

Kern glared at Murray. The twitch in the corner of his lip was back. "I don't know you, so don't get smart with me."

"I wouldn't dare get smart with you."

The chief's brow furrowed. "Sounds like you're still doing it."

The couple snickered from the couch again, and the lawman spun toward them. They remained in their embrace, though. Kern watched them for a moment as his lip twitched wildly. When his anger subsided, and his mouth stopped dancing, the chief glanced toward Murray's feet. "Where's your luggage?"

He could have said he had bags in his car, but that would have been easily disproved, either with a trip to the repair shop or a call to Waylon Forge. He knew better than to lie to an eager law enforcement officer. The truth was the best course to take.

"I don't have any."

"Don't have any? What's your name?"

"Murray."

Kern smirked. "Cute."

"Murray Lee."

"That's better. Where did you come from with no luggage, Murray Lee?"

Now, however, was the time to divert from the course of the truth. There was no way he would say Costa Buena, so he admitted to the last place he stopped. "Placerville."

"Where on God's green earth is that?"

"Near Sacramento."

"You drove up here, from Sacramento—"

"Placerville."

"—without any luggage. What would you do a thing like that for?"

"I heard about the festival," Murray said.

Kern's lip twitched. "The festival?"

"Yeah," Murray said with a nod. "I'm totally excited about it."

The chief glanced at Sebastian, who was now watching Murray with great interest.

"You like the movies?" the lawman asked.

"I love them. Edmund and Spartan." Murray lifted his chin toward the cutout in the corner. "Adela over there. The movies are simply beautiful. Life-changing, if you will."

"Everybody knows about those characters," the chief grumbled. He leaned into Murray. "You could have gone to McDonald's and seen their pictures on a jumbo cup."

Murray shrugged. "What about Rohan? Was he on a cup?"

"Rohan?" the lawman asked.

"The keeper of the wolves."

Kern grunted with displeasure. "You're one of them."

Murray smiled. "Lucky for me."

"I already said that," Sebastian said as he slid a room key across the counter.

Chapter 6

After Chief Kern left, Murray bypassed the elevator to take the stairs to the third floor.

He wasn't sure if the motif of his room aligned with the *Evenfall* movies or if it was just dated. He couldn't imagine a modern series of films looking like this, especially romantic vampire flicks.

Several cracks ran the length of the walls, and spackle covered minor dings.

Several large-framed pictures hung about the room. They were dark scenes of nature. One was a path entering a foreboding forest. Another was of a bear mauling a deer on the side of a mountain. And the final was of a dead squirrel.

Now, the original painter may not have intended them to be dark since they were amateurish. Together, however, their effect was unsettling even for a man who had spent most of his adult life dealing in humanity's darkness.

A threadbare spread covered a queen-sized bed, and the two pillows on top of it appeared lumpy.

In the corner of the room was a small round table made of dark wood that stood next to a chair covered in orange fabric.

A yellowed glass lamp hung in the corner of the ceiling; its brown power chord ran through a decorative chain to an outlet.

A greenish-blue shag carpet with wear patterns was underfoot.

It was as if the 1970s had come to visit but threw up all over the hotel room instead.

Waylon Forge had called the Belfry Boarding House cute as a bug. Now, Murray Lee was hoping it wouldn't have any.

After removing the postcards, he placed the plastic bag full of toiletries in the bathroom. Then he sat at the small table to write a couple of cryptic notes to Daphne Winterbourne, the woman he longed for who lived back in Pleasant Valley, Maine.

Murray needed to be careful with what he wrote, but he wanted to let her know he was okay and safe. He also wanted to tell her that he still thought about her. It only took a few minutes to scratch out the postcards.

When he finished, he realized he'd forgotten to buy postage stamps while at the pharmacy. He would do that tomorrow, he decided. What else was he going to do? It sounded like he would have plenty of time to kill over the next couple of days. He slid the postcards to the side and stood.

Murray crossed his arms and considered his position. He was a man without a country, a man without a family.

He couldn't call his grandmother, the only person he truly loved, and one of the main reasons he was able to be turned by the FBI. He wondered how she was doing. Wondering and worrying for too long would lead him to do something stupid. He had to push those thoughts from his head.

Next, he wondered what happened to Marshal Ted Onderdonk. The operator said he was *indisposed*. That could mean anything, especially in the coded world of the feds. Maybe the man was in the bathroom. Wouldn't she have told him that and arranged for some sort of call back?

And what about FBI Agent Max Ekleberry? He was the man who put him into this fix. Okay, that wasn't true. Murray put himself into this trouble with his choices, but Ekleberry was the guy who capitalized on those choices. Even so, the agent was turning out to be a decent guy. Ekleberry had come to his aid in Costa Buena. He could use some of that help right now.

It was odd for him to think of a couple of lawmen in favorable terms. Maybe as strange as it was for him to pine away for a woman that he barely even kissed.

Murray Lee shook the various thoughts from his head. He was a man of action, so overthinking tended not to help him.

He grabbed *The Deep Blue Good-by* and took a position on the bed. When he last had the book, he was in Maine. He'd almost finished it before he fled the town. Murray flipped through the book to find a section he hadn't read, and then he worked backward to a portion he recalled. He was further along than he remembered.

A sense of satisfaction filled him as he returned to the first adventure of Travis McGee.

Chapter 7

Pounding at the door caused him to wake and bolt upright. *The Deep Blue Good-by* tumbled from his chest to the floor.

As the thudding continued, he rubbed his face several times.

"Open up, Mr. Lee!" a male voice yelled from the hallway.

Murray was still in the clothes he'd arrived in, as he'd fallen asleep in them after finishing the book. He swung his legs off the bed and crossed the room in a few steps. He yanked open the door to find Chief Kern along with Officer Colton.

"What's going—"

As he entered, Kern put his hand on Murray's chest and pushed him backward. Colton slipped behind the chief and moved deeper into the room.

"Slow down," Murray said, "where's your warrant?"

"This is my warrant." The chief tapped his badge.

There wasn't anything illegal for them to find in his room, so Murray wasn't concerned about getting into trouble. The simple fact that two policemen were there is what made him feel immediately uncomfortable. And to think that the previous night he was having good feelings about two other lawmen.

Life has a funny way of putting things back into its proper perspective.

Murray lifted his hands in surrender. "Whatever."

"Now, you're learning," Chief Kern said.

"Look around if you want. I've got no problem with it."

"That's funny," Kern said, "because we got a problem with you."

"How's that?"

The chief snapped his fingers. "Let's see your driver's license."

From his back pocket, Murray reluctantly pulled out his wallet. He extracted his license and handed it to the lawman.

The chief lifted the license to the side of Murray's head to compare the picture to his actual face. He said to Colton. "You already took this info down, right?"

The officer looked back over his shoulder, nodded once, then returned to his search.

Kern lowered the license and flicked the edge of it with a finger from his free hand. "Says here you're Murray Lee."

"That's what I told you last night. Him, too. I wasn't trying to hide it."

"Then who's Owen Hunter?"

Murray blinked before saying the only thing he could think of at that moment. "What?"

The chief grinned. "The car you left at Forge's? That car doesn't belong to you. We did a DMV check and confirmed it belongs to some guy named Owen Hunter."

Crud, Murray thought. When Onderdonk established his new identity, he must not have transferred over the vehicle to match. That could—no, it *did*—create a problem. "Owen is a friend."

"Really?"

Murray slowly nodded.

"Do you know what we found when we ran Owen's name?" Kern asked. "Don't bother guessing. I'll tell you. We found a law enforcement flag from the Costa Buena Police Department. There's a detective down there who wants to talk with your buddy concerning a murder. We've got a call into him to find out what's going on."

"They handled it," Murray said.

"Handled?" the chief asked. His eyes flicked to Officer Colton, then back to Murray. "How's that?"

"It was a misunderstanding. They arrested the actual murderer, so Owen is no longer a suspect. They forgot to remove the tag, is all. Probably a bureaucratic snafu. You know how those things go."

"You sure know a lot about your friend," Kern said.

"Yeah," Colton offered in support while he looked under the bed. He saw *The Deep Blue Good-by* on the floor and tossed it up onto the nightstand.

"We're close," Murray said, holding up two crossed fingers. "Like brothers."

The chief rubbed his chin. "We'll see if that rings true when that detective calls me back. But for now, I think you're full of it."

Murray's two crossed fingers unhooked, and he raised his hand higher as if he were swearing-in before a judge. "I'm telling the truth."

"Maybe if we knew how to get a hold of your buddy, Owen, we could feel better about things. Otherwise, we're likely to suspect you took the man's car without asking."

"Why would I do that?"

Kern shrugged. "Because you seem like the untrustworthy type."

"I do?"

The chief nodded. "Tattoos and unshaven."

Murray's face flattened, and he ran his hand over his scratchy chin. "I just woke up."

"And the tattoos appeared overnight, too. Sort of like your bad breath?"

"No," he said. "Obviously."

"See my dilemma? So, how do we get in touch with your good ol' pal, Owen?"

Murray hadn't been in this situation before, and he wasn't sure what to do. He could give them the name of the record store that he ran while living under the pseudonym Owen Hunter, but if they called it and no one answered, what would they do then? Would the chief continue to harass him? He was going to be stuck on this island for a few days until the bridge reopened, or he got off by boat.

There was only one phone number he knew, so he decided to give that to them.

"Call him at his job," Murray said.

"Where's that?"

"Ace Adventures."

Colton moved to the small round table and moved the postcards apart. He flipped both over. Murray tried to remember what he wrote to Daphne.

"What's that?" Kern asked. "Ace Adventures?"

"A travel agency," Murray muttered.

"And what's your friend do there?"

"He's an operator," Murray said.

Officer Colton's brow furrowed as he studied the postcards. His lips moved as he read what Murray had written to Daphne.

"An operator?" Kern asked.

"You know," Murray said, glancing at the chief, "he takes calls. Try him there, but you have to ask for him by name since you never know who will answer the phone. He doesn't have a direct line."

"What's the number?" Kern asked.

Murray rattled off the digits, and the chief wrote them in his notebook.

Colton asked Murray, "Why'd you sign these postcards with the initials BS?"

The chief walked over to stand next to Colton. He grabbed one of the postcards. "Daphne? Is that your girlfriend?"

"You need a warrant," Murray said weakly.

"Pleasant Valley, Maine," the chief muttered as he continued to read the card.

"The initials," Colton insisted. "What do they mean?"

"It's a code."

The chief's eyes narrowed. "Code for what?"

Murray inhaled deeply before saying, "Beautifully sweet."

Colton's lip curled. "You signed it, Beautifully Sweet?"

His heart began to race. When he said beautifully sweet, he was thinking of Daphne, but the initials were supposed to be for him. He'd made a mistake by opening his mouth. He wasn't about to do it again, so he remained silent.

The chief studied Murray. "Did she give you that nickname or something?"

"Something like that," he muttered.

Kern glanced at Colton, and the two men both scrunched their noses. "Dumb," they said simultaneously and started laughing.

Murray crossed his arms. "Did you come here this morning just to bust my chops?"

The chief tossed his postcard to the table. "There was another attack on a local last night. Miss Welford was bitten and robbed."

"Is she okay?" Murray asked.

"Nice of you to be worried," the chief said. "Louise is fine. The bites aren't that bad, to tell the truth, so she's well enough to describe her attacker." Kern pointed at Murray. "He sounded a lot like you."

"Which was?"

"Big and ugly."

Murray smirked. "Cute."

"And wearing a hat," Officer Colton said. He held up the green John Deere baseball hat.

"It's raining," Murray said. "Lots of people wear hats in this weather."

"Actually," the officer said, "most visitors to the island right now aren't hat types. They tend toward the umbrella. It's more elegant. Plus, they don't want their make-up or glitter getting ruined."

Kern eyed Murray with suspicion. "You don't seem to be too worried about your make-up."

"Or your glitter," Colton added.

Murray frowned.

"That's two attacks," the chief said, holding up as many fingers, "in one night. The same night as you showed up. Neat coincidence."

"There's a lot of people on this island. I'm not exactly the type who's going to bite, now am I?"

"How do we know?" Colton said. "Maybe you're doing it to throw us off the trail. Getting us to look at the fans of the movies."

Kern snapped his fingers and pointed to his officer. "Right."

"Haven't people tried to bite other people before?" Murray asked. "Waylon mentioned something of the sort. So did Pam at the pharmacy."

The chief shook his head. "It's a vampire festival. Of course, people are going to try to bite others. It's vampire nature, but no one has ever done it in connection to a robbery. That's a new twist. That's why we're looking at you."

Murray glanced between the two men. "Now that you've been in my room, I take it you didn't find whatever was stolen from either Mrs. Welford or Abner Dewey."

Kern looked at Colton, who shook his head in return.

"I'm in the clear now?" Murray asked.

The chief sighed, then reluctantly shrugged.

Murray needed to give the officers a reasonable way out, or they'd stick around longer in hopes of connecting him to these crimes. So he said, "After you checked my car and found it registered to someone else, you got worried I wasn't who I said I was."

Both Kern and Colton nodded.

"That's what happened," the chief said.

A chill suddenly ran up Murray's back as a new thought occurred to him.

Did they only run the license plate, or did they search his car?

The envelope with his new cover story was still inside the glove box. Did they get inside, or had they only looked at his car from the outside? And if they did get inside, had they opened the glove box? If so, did they miss it in his search? Could he be so fortunate?

"It was reasonable for us to look at you," Kern said. "Especially since you're not here for the festival. You kind of stick out when compared to everyone else."

Murray politely nodded. It was better to agree with the cops rather than argue with them. Most lawmen liked it when they believed they were the smartest people in a room.

Kern lightly smacked Colton with the back of his hand. "Let's go. We've still got work to do."

The officer turned and left the hotel room.

The chief paused before stepping into the hallway. "A word to the wise, Mr. Lee."

"What's that?"

"Whatever you're into—"

"Who says I'm into anything?"

Kern held up his hand. "Save it. There's an air about you that's foul with secrets. So whatever you're into, I don't want it in my town. I like things I can understand. When the bridge opens, I want you to get in your car and find your way out of here."

"I haven't done anything."

"Yet."

"What if I don't go?" Murray shouldn't have asked it, but he didn't like feeling pushed around.

Kern grinned. "Hang around and see what happens. There's nothing I like better than laying down the law."

Without waiting for Murray to respond, the chief turned and left the room.

Murray stood alone and wondered what he'd done wrong in this small town to upset the police chief.

If he believed in such a thing, he might just think it was karma trying to balance things out. Now that he was working to be a decent person, maybe the universe was going to pay him back for all the bad things he'd done in life.

He shook that thought from his head and headed toward the shower.

Chapter 8

Light rain continued to fall as he walked up Main Street. He felt foolish using the yellow umbrella again, but at least the rest of the festival crowd used them, too. It rested against his shoulder in a relaxed, almost fashionable way. He'd never used one before and for a good reason. He always thought they weren't manly, tough, or cool. However, he was dry this morning. For that, he was thankful.

Maybe being manly, tough, or cool was overrated, he thought. It was a new idea and felt alien to him.

A young man and woman approached him from the opposite end of the block. They walked closely together under a large blue umbrella. The two were both sharply dressed in tailored suits. His was silver, and hers was gray. The left sides of their faces glittered. Once near, their expressions slackened, and they exhibited the disaffected looks he now associated with the cinematic vampires. They were living examples of the cardboard cutouts.

After they passed, the couple giggled maliciously. He turned to watch them hug tighter under their canopy. From behind, the man's thin frame closely matched that of the woman's, and their hips swung in unison. They chattered wildly and glanced back at Murray with wicked glee.

At that moment, he considered a simple life principle. It was so straightforward that it should have been a foregone conclusion, yet he had just doubted it.

His pursuit of being a better person should not cause him to throw away inescapable truths even if he'd discovered them during his former life—a time full of crime. Just because he learned a lesson during a firestorm of bad decisions didn't make it any less useful. He could and should still embrace it and hold on to it, for those lessons were learned the hard way.

Murray's face warmed, his eyes narrowed, and his jaw set. The nattily dressed couple stopped their snickering and turned away. They sashayed farther down the sidewalk.

The truth of the matter was this—being manly, tough, or cool was never overrated, and it would never go out of style.

He snapped the yellow umbrella closed and let the rain wet his baseball cap and jacket. Murray thought about hurrying up behind the glittering man, spinning him around, and punching the snickering nitwit in the mouth. Doing that, however, was not cool and was most definitely not the action of a better man.

Besides, it would call too much attention to himself and violate one of the essential rules that Marshal Onderdonk had set for him.

Do not contact people from your old life.
Do not visit places from your old life.
Do not develop habits from your old life.

Violence was most certainly a habit from his old life. Learning restraint, no matter how inconvenient, would keep him on the path to finding the better person inside him.

His rumbling stomach dragged him from his internal struggle for petty payback. He glanced around for a restaurant and found one nearby—the Belfry Bruncheonette.

It was a small establishment laden with green and brown hues. The clientele was mostly silver-haired. At first, the average age of the patrons didn't bother him as he searched for an open seat. Then his pulse quickened, and he froze. He scanned the restaurant again, but this time he looked for purple hats. Finding none, he relaxed and let out an audible sigh.

There was only one open seat at the end of the counter. Unfortunately, it was next to a cardboard cutout of a skinny man in a sheriff's uniform. Murray took the seat while the flat lawman eyed him with suspicion.

"Something to drink?" A waitress in a brown T-shirt and blue jeans slid a menu in front of Murray. The name tag on her uniform read *Georgia.*

He jerked his head toward the cutout. "Who's that?"

Georgia frowned at the life-size portrait. "Sheriff Ryser. You don't know who that is?"

Murray shook his head and leaned back to study the perpetually stiff lawman.

"He's Adela's father," Georgia said. "Kind of a wasted character, you ask me. The guy is supposed to be the sheriff of the island. We don't have a sheriff in real life, but I guess that's what they call creative license."

"Sure."

The server eyed the cutout. "Adela moves to Belfry so she can live with him, but the guy is a goof. He spends the whole series pining away for an ex-wife who has moved on. She's a flighty one, by the way. The guy should be happy he got away from her. And while he's got his head up his you-know-what, he never connects with his daughter. She runs around on this whole big adventure with werewolves and vampires, and he just bumbles away. Dear old dad is a schlub."

"Schlub?"

"Schmuck. I mean, the guy is supposed to be the sheriff—"

"Which Belfry doesn't have."

"Yet, the guy can't find a hole in a box full of donuts."

"Sounds like most cops."

Georgia rolled her eyes. "Most cops are smarter than that. As a character, though, the dad is wasted. But what can you expect? It's supposed to be a teenage girl's fantasy."

"To hang out with the undead?"

She smirked. "To be the center of attention. For everyone to tell her she's beautiful and smart. Ugh. It's so stupid."

"I take it you didn't move here for the movies?"

Georgia spread her arms wide. "Born and raised here. Probably die here, too."

"You sound like a John Mellencamp song."

"I think I know that one."

He pushed the menu aside and ordered a couple of eggs, hash browns, a cup of coffee, and a banana to go.

"Banana to go?"

"A snack."

She shrugged and walked off to give the cook his order. While she was gone, he scanned the restaurant. No one inside appeared to be dressed up in celebration of the movie. There were no glittering faces, and no one wore tailored suits. In fact, no one was dressed up at all.

He then surveyed the establishment itself. There were no pictures from the movie. There were some old black and white photos of Belfry but nothing that even hinted at the film series, except the cardboard cutout of Adela's father.

When Georgia returned, she slipped a cup of coffee in front of him. "If you're not here for the festival, what brought you to town?"

"Wrong turn."

"Heck of a turn, especially before the bridge goes out."

"This place," he said, glancing about the restaurant, "and these folks. They don't seem to go for the movies."

"They don't," she said and checked the patrons along with him.

"So, not everyone was excited about the movies filming here?"

"Most were in favor of them before they blew up into this silly madness." She pointed at the cardboard sheriff.

"If you don't like the movies," Murray asked, "why have one of those cutouts?"

"We have to," she said and shrugged. "It's a civic thing. Chamber of Commerce, you know? Anyway, we insist on the sheriff every year, which no one ever fights us for."

"Why is that?"

"Because the fans don't care about him. Like most teenage girls and their fathers."

"I wouldn't know. I was never a teenaged girl."

She smiled. "All the fans want is to get their pictures taken with Edmund and Spartan and Adela."

"What about Rohan?"

Her eyes slanted. "I didn't think you were a fan."

"I've picked up some info by walking around town. But you've watched the films?"

Georgia nodded. "Sure."

"Why watch them if you didn't support them?"

"I'm human, and I'm curious, but once was enough, thank you very much."

"Did you read the books?" He leaned forward and said in a conspiratorial voice, "I hear they're better than the movies."

Georgia laughed. "Uh, no. I tried to read the first one, but it was awful. So much unnecessary drama filled every page. I was a teenager once. I don't ever want to be one again."

"Even with the chance of being swept away by a glittery vampire?"

"Especially not that."

Murray sipped his coffee. "Have you heard about the attacks around town?"

"The biting?"

He nodded. "What do you think of that?"

"Not sure what to make of it. Maybe someone likes the movies too much."

"You don't seem worried about it, though."

She shrugged. "What are we going to do? The bites don't seem too bad, and they're only robbing our upper crust."

"Upper crust?"

Georgia nodded. "Ol' Abner Dewey got robbed of a watch. He was in earlier this morning to tell his story. Abner shows that watch off all the time. I'm surprised someone hasn't taken it sooner. And Miss Louise Welford—" Georgia nodded toward a gray-haired woman sitting with a couple of other ladies. "She was robbed last night after she locked up her store."

Louise had a bandage on her neck, and she absently touched it as she spoke to her dining companions.

"What store does Mrs. Welford own?"

"That's Miss Welford. Don't get that wrong, or she'll never let you forget. She's never been married and is not afraid to let you know that miss applies to unmarried women as well as the young."

Murray glanced back at the chatty silver-haired woman.

Georgia whispered. "She's got the little hobby store at the end of the block. If you meet her, you're in for a treat."

A bell dinged from the kitchen, and Georgia hurried away.

At that moment, Louise and her friends stood to leave. The three older women passed behind him on their way out of the restaurant.

"Here you go," Georgia said, carefully placing a platter onto the counter.

Murray examined his breakfast and lifted his fork.

"You should go to the bonfire tonight," Georgia said.

"Why?"

"Where else can you see a hundred people on a beach dancing around a fire?"

Murray nodded and stuck his fork into his hash browns. He paused and looked up at her. "Wait. Doesn't fire hurt vampires?"

"In the movie, the bonfire was a scene with the werewolves—"

"Lycans."

Georgia squinted. "You sure you didn't watch the movies?"

"I was already corrected about my misuse of the term by Pam over at the pharmacy."

"Pam," she said with a dismissive shake. "She does love the wolfies, doesn't she? Anyway, since nobody has the body or the confidence to walk around shirtless, the townies co-opted the bonfire. That's when we all go down and celebrate the festival. Most of the vampire wannabes stay away and, if you want the truth, that's okay with us."

Murray shoved some hash browns in his mouth.

"So you'll come by?" Georgia asked.

He nodded and mumbled "maybe" through a mouthful of food.

Chapter 9

After breakfast, he walked to the end of the block and found Batty for Crafts, Louise Welford's store. It was still closed and wouldn't be open for a couple of hours. While he waited, he decided to check on the status of his car.

The Toyota was inside the first bay with its hood propped up. Even with the roll-door open and a light rain outside, the garage smelled of grease and gas.

A radio blared in the corner. Waylon Forge leaned over the side panel and mumbled along with Elton John's "Don't Let the Sun Go Down on Me." He wore the same brown beanie and faded overalls he had on the day before.

When Murray asked, "What do you think—" Waylon jumped and hit his head on the underside of the hood.

The shop owner turned angrily to Murray and, with a wrench still in his hand, rubbed his head. "Dadgummit, son. What'd you go and do that for?"

"Mighty jumpy this morning."

Waylon rubbed his head a final time before resting a hip against the car. "People are getting bitten around here. Man's gotta be a little more aware at a time like this."

"That's what you were? Aware?"

Waylon's eyes went to the ceiling.

Wrecker limped out of the office then. His mouth hung open in his toothy grin. He leaned against Murray, and the big man petted the side of the dog's head.

The shop owner tapped the wrench into his open palm. "You here for something specific or just to test my reflexes?"

Murray jerked his head toward the car. "Find the problem?"

Waylon slowly nodded and leaned over the engine. "Looks to be your oxygen sensor."

"You don't sound convinced."

"Finding the problem is one thing."

"But fixing it is another?"

Waylon nodded. "I don't have the part on hand. We've got to get to the mainland and get a new sensor from there."

"Can't you order it on-line? Have it shipped in?"

Waylon straightened and stared at Murray as if he were explaining math to Wrecker.

"The bridges," Murray finally said. His face warmed with embarrassment.

"You ain't too smart, are you?" the shop owner said.

"I get it," he said.

"How can the mailman get us the part if we can't get over the bridges?"

"I get it," Murray repeated.

"I mean, it's not like we have an airport on this island. Maybe we can have a drone fly in your oxygen sensor, all special like." Waylon spread his arms wide and buzzed his lips together like an airplane engine.

"I get it."

Waylon chuckled. "Maybe they could bring it over by boat once the rain settles and the river calms." Murray started to respond, but Waylon said, "You get it, yeah, yeah, I know. So you're stuck here, along with the rest of us, until the bridge reopens. Once that happens, I'll run over to the parts store, grab a new sensor, and get you up and running."

Murray crossed his arms.

"Unless," Waylon said, "you can find someone on the island to give up their oxygen sensor."

He felt a moment of hope, and his spirits brightened considerably. "Know anyone with this type of car on the island?"

Waylon stepped back to appraise the dented Toyota Tercel. "Not many people proudly drive this type of vehicle anymore."

"It's a classic," Murray said half-heartedly.

"If you say so."

A police car raced by with its lights and sirens activated. The scanner on the shelf inside the office squawked to life.

"Colton, where are you?"

"Here, Chief. What's up?"

"Meet me at the station. I want to talk about these robberies."

"What's this town coming to?" Waylon muttered.

"Did the chief come to see you this morning?"

Waylon nodded. "He did. The man wanted to know about you."

"What did you tell him?"

"What could I? I said you dropped off your car last night and that I was going to start work on it today. Not much more to tell."

"Did he search the inside of it?"

"He wanted to," Waylon said, "but I wouldn't allow it. I told him he needed a warrant for such a thing."

"And he listened to you?"

"Of course he did. He knows the law."

Murray frowned. Kern knew the law all right, and he also knew who he could push around and who he couldn't. "I need to get inside my car," Murray said.

Waylon waved toward the Toyota. "Help yourself. It's yours."

Murray walked around to the passenger side and dropped into the seat. When the glove box flopped open, he immediately noticed the envelope was missing.

When he fled Costa Buena, Marshal Onderdonk handed him an envelope. It contained a driver's license, a thousand dollars in cash, and a printout.

While in Eureka, he checked out his new identity. He almost had a fit when he saw his newly assigned name. It was clear Onderdonk was getting even for Murray blowing two covers. The first name he'd received sounded like an action movie star—Brody Steele. The second name was that of an accountant—Owen Hunter.

But *Murray?*

Murray was a poodle's name.

Unfortunately, beggars can't be choosers.

He put the new license into his wallet and burned the old one. He stuffed the money into his pockets. But he only gave a passing glance to the printout. It wasn't long enough to internalize any of its information.

The marshals had added a military back story—a little time in the Navy—but he didn't see what he'd done in the service. His new cover was arrested a few times for things like malicious mischief and assault, but he hadn't paid attention to where and when.

Murray had thought he would have plenty of time later to memorize it all. He should have made learning his new back story a priority, and then he should have destroyed the document.

Now it was missing.

Murray poked his head out of the car. "You sure the chief wasn't in here?"

"He never got in it," Waylon said. "I promise."

"What about his officer?"

"Caleb? Him neither. No one got in your car. Both of them walked around it and looked in through the windows. The chief wrote down your license plate. But that's all they did."

If that was true, what happened to the envelope? He flipped through the items in the glove box again and realized the vehicle's registration was also missing.

"What about you?" Murray asked as he stepped from the vehicle. "You got in the car to drive it into the shop."

"I got in. Yeah."

"There was an envelope in the glove box along with the registration."

Waylon tapped his wrench into his hand. "What are you suggesting?"

"I'm not suggesting anything. I'm only asking if you found an envelope."

The shop owner stepped into the office, and Murray followed. Wrecker limped along behind them.

Once inside, Waylon lifted a clipboard from his desk and held it shoulder high. Underneath the clapper was a white envelope. "You mean this?"

Murray's pulse quickened. "That's it."

Waylon yanked the envelope free of the clapper. "This is the darnedest thing I've ever seen."

"How's that?"

The shop owner studied Murray before saying, "Inside this little envelope is sort of a history of your life. Childhood, military service, run-ins with the law. Not necessarily interesting reading, but you boiled your whole life down to a few pages."

Murray swallowed, and his eyes locked onto the envelope in Waylon's dirty hand.

"It's almost as if you're trying to remember your own story."

Hoping to calm himself, he took a deep breath and held it. He needed to come up with a plausible reason for having a synopsis of Murray Lee's life in his glove box.

Less is more, he thought. If he said too much, he would paint himself into a corner.

Waylon spoke before he could talk, though. "You didn't take a wrong turn onto Belfry Island, did you?"

And there it was. The shop owner knew he was lying. The more people who knew Murray's identity was a lie, the more trouble he was going to have.

Time was running out, so he had to decide on a course of action quickly.

Murray's hands curled into fists.

Should he attack Waylon and take the envelope back? That's what Beauregard Smith would have done. He would have done it with a violence of action and without any remorse. However, Beau Smith wasn't here. Murray Lee was.

And Murray Lee wanted to be better than his predecessor.

Besides, he was stuck on the small island. If he hit the older man, where would he go? Hiding places would be limited, and Chief Kern and Officer Colton would soon track him down. Cornered on Belfry Island was not how he wanted his freedom to come to an end.

"You can tell me, son," Waylon said. His voice was soft. "You came to sell your story, didn't you?"

"What are you talking about?"

"No need to pretend. I'm not judging. You're trying to find an agent for your book idea, aren't you?" He waved the envelope. "All sorts of agents and authors attend this festival. Most of them want to sell the next fantasy blockbuster. I've even thought about pitching an idea or two, but I'm just an ol' mechanic with a tepid imagination." He cocked his head at Murray. "You didn't think I would know a word like that, did you? Tepid. It means mild, in case you're wondering."

"I wasn't."

"Anyway," Waylon continued, "I ain't never heard of anyone selling a biography like yours while at the festival, but who knows? Buck the trend."

Waylon extended his hand and gave the envelope to Murray. The shop owner patted his shoulder as he passed by on the way back into the garage. "I wish you the best of luck, my friend, but can I give you some advice?"

"What's that?" Murray asked.

Waylon pointed to the envelope. "You should ditch the biography idea. Your past reads sort of boring."

Murray's eyes fell to the envelope covered with dirty handprints.

"I read through that twice," the old man continued, "and you've never been in too much trouble, nor been in too much excitement. At least, that's how it looks to me. Maybe you could embellish your history. Add some spice to your life. Otherwise, people ain't gonna be too interested in reading it." Waylon scratched underneath his beanie with the wrench. "And for as tough as you look, I would have thought you did something more exciting than being a boatswain's mate in the Navy. But who am I to judge? I was a cook in the Coast Guard."

Murray had no idea what a boatswain's mate was, but Waylon Forge seemed to think the concept was funny.

He tucked the envelope into his back pocket and left the auto shop.

Chapter 10

It took about twenty minutes for him to walk to the edge of the old bridge, the one he had crossed yesterday. On the Belfry side, there were several white sawhorses with red-painted two by fours crisscrossed over each other to form giant Xs.

Fifty feet in front of the sawhorses were orange caution cones. Another sawhorse held a hand-painted sign that read *Bridge Out—Do Not Attempt to Cross—Life Endangering.*

Murray walked to the edge of the road and watched the water flow over the top of the bridge. The wooden structure moaned and creaked as it stood helplessly in the middle of the rushing river. Water pushed against its eastern side before some cascaded over, and the rest ran under before it all raced farther west to the Pacific Ocean.

He shoved his hands into his jacket as rain clung to the brim of his hat. The droplets seemed to be a little heavier now.

Murray looked across to the mainland, where a group of leather-clad men huddled together. Nearby, a row of motorcycles stood proudly in a row. He couldn't make out their faces, but even from this distance, Murray knew who they were—the Satan's Dawgs.

No one else waited at the water's edge, eager for an opportunity to pass into Belfry. Most Evenfall fans probably came early. Maybe the room he got at the boarding house was for someone who ended up sick and couldn't attend the festival at all.

A commotion erupted among the group as one of them pointed at Murray. He leaned forward to see what they were doing.

A small tree near him exploded a moment before the sound registered.

Thunk!

Then several *thwips* occurred as bullets ripped through the leaves of the nearby trees.

Murray hunched, a reflexive action one makes when ducking for cover. The man across the water wasn't pointing at him; he was aiming a gun. The shooting didn't last long, though.

Another of the leather-clad men smacked the gunman's arm, which caused the weapon to drop to the ground. The two men briefly argued until the larger one slapped the former gunman and pointed to the row of motorcycles. The smaller man trundled over to a bike, climbed on, and rode away.

The larger man stepped forward to the water's edge now. It was then that Murray could make him out.

His name was Keaton Scoville, but inside the club, he'd earned the title of The Bloodhound. He wasn't a killer. He was a tracker.

Scoville had previously found several people who had crossed the Satan's Dawgs. When he discovered them, he turned their locations over to the man Murray used to be. It never ended well for those the Bloodhound tracked.

Keaton Scoville cupped his hands around his mouth and yelled, but Murray couldn't hear the words over the rushing water and drizzling rain.

He held his hand to his ear, and Scoville yelled louder. It didn't matter, though. He still couldn't hear. Murray shrugged and exaggeratedly shook his head.

Scoville understood the meaning of Murray's mime, so he waved toward the group of men he was with before touching his chest. Then he pointed across the river to Murray.

Yeah, Murray thought. *You're coming to get me. I already know.*

Then Keaton Scoville slowly dragged his hand across his throat.

I know that, too, Murray thought.

The Bloodhound waved goodbye to Murray before returning to the pack of Dawgs.

Chapter 11

Murray started toward downtown but detoured to the opposite side of the island. Waylon Forge had said he could get off the island by boat. Perhaps that was what he should do now—find a way off that didn't require him to wait for the bridge to reopen.

It was evident the Satan's Dawgs weren't going to be discouraged by the poor weather. They would wait out the storm and enter Belfry when the river calmed.

Perhaps Murray could find someone with a boat and get across the water. Washington State was on the north side of the Columbia River. If he made it across, he could catch a bus to someplace safe. Or maybe he could hitchhike to safety.

Neither of those options sounded particularly appealing, though.

Being on a bus was a bad idea. They were slow and clumsy vehicles, and he had no control over the route. A group of motorcycle-riding Dawgs would easily catch him.

Hitchhiking was a worse idea. It put him entirely in the open. With his thumb humiliatingly extended, no less.

Perhaps he should steal a car after he made it into Washington State.

And get arrested for Grand Theft Auto, he thought ruefully. Or whatever they called stealing cars in that state.

Getting pinched would land him in jail where brothers of the Satan's Dawgs would no doubt be. But if he were in prison, Marshal Onderdonk would at least be able to find him and get him out.

Would he, though?

Would Onderdonk pull Murray out of jail? Had he already used up his last favor in Costa Buena? Onderdonk didn't want to burn the first cover, which had been in use less than a week while in Maine. That made two covers in the garbage in less than a month.

His was not a good start to life in witness protection.

And the idea of Onderdonk helping him might be moot, anyway. Murray didn't even know if the marshal was okay. What happened to him after Murrary fled Costa Buena? For all he knew, the man could be dead. It was a sobering thought and one he didn't want to linger on for too long. He didn't want to trust the feds any more than he had to, but he had built a begrudging respect for Onderdonk. He wanted the man to be all right.

Twenty minutes later, Murray found himself on the north side of the little island. The Columbia River looked rough. There were large whitecaps on the water as it bounced and chopped every which way.

As he watched the river, he pulled the banana from his pocket. He slowly ate the fruit as he searched up and down the river. Untold minutes passed by, and he never saw a boat. It didn't look safe enough for anyone to cross to the Washington side. He didn't need to risk his life today. Maybe another day, but not this one.

He tossed the banana peel into some bushes and continued.

Murray walked along Shoreline Road as it curved away from the water. A rock fence portioned off the remaining land. From a distance, he could see a large home sitting proudly in the middle of this homestead. It was much larger than any other he'd seen so far on the island. As he neared an opening in the fence, a driveway led up to the house.

Affixed to the column on the west side of the driveway was a brass plate. It read Dewey. On the opposite column, a black mailbox hung.

Up near the house, a pickup started.

Murray thought about walking by, but he paused.

The truck—a dented 1980s rig—drove slowly along the windy driveway. When it neared the opening in the fence line, the pickup stopped. The driver's door opened, and an older man got out. Tinny country music came from the inside of the cab.

He took one step toward the mailbox, then paused. From across the hood, the older man eyed Murray. "Help you?" he asked.

"Are you Abner Dewey?"

"Who's asking?"

Murray walked around the truck and extended his hand. "Murray Lee."

Taped to the man's neck was white gauze. He wore a flannel shirt, blue jeans, and brown work boots. His head was bald on top, with thin wisps of gray hair on the sides.

The man was a foot shorter than Murray. Abner Dewey ignored the extended hand, which caused Murray to pull it back.

"What do you want?"

"Nothing," Murray said. "Being friendly is all. I heard you got bit."

"People talk too much."

"It's the talk of the town."

Abner smirked, then continued to his mailbox. Before he yanked open the little door, he muttered, "Darn kids."

"Think it was a kid?"

The older man glanced back at Murray. "Everyone's a kid to me. 'Sides, I got robbed *and* bit. Does that sound like something a grown—" Abner bent over and stuck his hand into the mailbox. "—man would do?" He removed a handful of envelopes then slapped the lid shut.

"What did your attacker look like?"

Abner faced Murray and frowned. "You some sort of police?"

"Concerned citizen."

"Don't see many of them around these days. You must be new to the island."

"Just visiting."

Abner's lip curled, and his eyes narrowed. "For the festival."

"Do I look like someone who wears glitter?"

That quieted the smirk on the older man's lips.

"So, was he big?" Murray asked.

Abner considered the question for a moment, then nodded.

"As big as me?"

"Heaven's no," Abner said, "but it doesn't take much to be bigger than me."

"Chief Kern said you described your attacker as ugly."

The older man seemed taken aback. "I never said that. They attacked me from the rear. I never got a good look at them."

"They?" Murray asked.

Abner's eyes narrowed. "He. Him."

"If he attacked you from the rear, then how did you know he was big?"

The older man leaned into his truck to put the mail on the seat. While inside, the tinny country music abruptly ended. When he repositioned himself outside of the pickup, Abner said, "Son, when someone big is behind you, you know. Ever have anyone grab you from behind?"

He had.

"What did he sound like?" Murray asked.

"Sound like?"

"Yeah. How was his voice? Low, high. Did he have an accent?"

Abner seemed uncomfortable with the question. "He tried to disguise it. Sometimes it was low. Sometimes he tried an accent."

"So you couldn't get a read on it?"

"You've got a lot of questions," the older man grumbled. "This leading somewhere?"

An idea tinkled in the back of Murray's mind. "I heard they took a watch."

The older man crossed his arms. "You hear a lot for someone who ain't the police."

"I assume it was valuable."

Abner Dewey studied Murray for a moment. When he decided something for himself, he pursed his lips and nodded.

"What was it worth?" Murray asked.

"In real money?" Abner chuckled. "Heck, I don't know. About fifteen thousand, maybe. It was my father's Rolex." Abner extended his left arm to reveal a bare wrist. "But in sentimental value, it was worth much more than that."

"What'd Chief Kern say?"

"Martin? He and that flunky of his didn't say much. They took a report, but they didn't get none too excited about finding it."

"Because it's small."

"That's right."

"And it will be hard to find."

"Uh-huh. Kern said they'd look, but it's a small department." A mixture of sadness and frustration crossed Abner's face. "I'm going to have to get used to not having it anymore. It's the only thing I had left to remember my father, God rest his soul. I lost everything else in a fire about twenty years ago. I escaped with the clothes on my back and the watch around my wrist. Insurance will replace a lot of things, but it won't replace a family heirloom."

Hearing about the insurance company turned the tinkle at the back of his mind into a full-on clang. The bells quieted as Murray's thoughts moved to *The Deep Blue Good-by*, Travis McGee, and his situation.

He was stuck on the island for at least another day. There was no way for him to get off unless he could charter a boat to cross the rough water, and that didn't seem safe. Sitting around worrying about what *might* happen when the Dawgs made it into Belfry would drive him crazy. There could be a way for him to distract himself until the bridge opened.

"What if I found the watch for you?" Murray asked.

Abner's eyes widened. "You know where it's at?" His hand reached up to touch the bandage at his neck. "You know the person who did this to me?"

"No," Murray said, "but I'm something of a salvage consultant." Saying the phrase Travis McGee called himself thrilled Murray in a way that uttering the word bookkeeper never did.

"What's that mean? Salvage consultant."

"It works like this, Mr. Dewey. You reported the watch stolen—"

The older man nodded.

"I'm assuming the insurance will cover the replacement cost."

Abner's eyes were slitted. "Most of it. Yeah."

"And you've already notified your insurance company?"

"I did this morning."

Murray's heart rate quickened. "Let's say I find the person who bit you."

"Okay. Let's say."

"And let's say I recover the watch."

The older man's eyes widened. "Keep saying."

"Well, you keep the insurance payout, but you give me a finder's fee."

"How much?"

"Half."

"Half?" Abner Dewey seemed genuinely offended.

"That seems about right for something as small and valuable as a father's watch."

Abner's lip curled as he thought. "You really think you can find it?"

Murray shrugged. "I don't know, but I'm stuck on this island until the bridge opens, and I got nothing better to do. It seems like a good use of my time, don't you think?"

The older man slowly nodded. "Probably better than pretending you're a vampire. What do we do now?"

"We shake on it."

Murray stuck out his hand, and Abner eyed it. When he clasped it, the older man said, "Okay, Mr. Lee. Let's see what you can do."

Chapter 12

It took him some time to return downtown. When he finally made it to the line of shops on Main Street, the rain had soaked his hat. His shoes were drenched, and the cuffs of his jeans were dark with moisture. His nylon jacket remained waterproof, however.

The wetness didn't bother Murray Lee and, surprisingly, no longer did his predicament of being stuck on Belfry Island. He stood straighter, and his stride seemed longer, for he now had a quest.

Having a purpose in life felt good.

It wasn't a grand reason, he knew, but even a small purpose was something important, considering his situation. Lamenting the poor life choices that led him to this place seemed like a waste of time. Instead, he could find a biting, robbing vampire and recover Abner Dewey's Rolex.

As a bonus, the latter sounded immensely more fun.

His hands were cramping from the cold and rain. He had intermittently shoved them into his pockets, but that only brought temporary relief. He stepped into the first shop he came to—an antique store with the name The Lost Toys—and was greeted with the blaring warmth of a heater turned on full blast.

As the door shut with an annoying clang, a head popped out from behind a curtained doorway. A moment later, the rest of the body wriggled out and moved toward the counter.

Murray stamped his feet before taking off his baseball hat. He smacked it against his leg in hopes of knocking any excess water off. After resetting the cap, he stepped farther into the store but stopped immediately.

Another life-sized cutout stood at the front near a collection of old magazines. She was an attractive pale woman who wore an expertly tailored plaid suit. Her short hair had a slight curl near her cheekbones. Her red eyes bore into Murray.

"Who's this?" Murray asked.

"That's Planaria," the shopkeeper growled.

"What kind of name is that? Planaria?"

"A vampire name." Contempt filled the man's voice.

Murray raised an eyebrow. "You don't like them?"

"The bloodsuckers? No."

"Why do you have this in your store, then?"

"The Chamber of Commerce says we gotta have one. Just like these stupid name tags." He flicked a piece of plastic attached to his T-shirt. "On the bright side, the actress is pretty. And the vampire she's pretending to be isn't real."

The store owner straightened, moved around the counter, then ambled toward him. He had long hair that fell to his shoulders and more than a day's worth of splotchy stubble on his chin. His faded blue jeans had tears at the knees, and his checkered Vans were dirty. His

T-shirt featured a menacing frog in the middle of a circle. Around the edge of its logo, the shirt read *Frog Brothers Comics, Santa Carla, California.*

On the left side of his shirt was clipped a plastic name tag that read *Welcome to Belfry.* Underneath the welcome statement was printed *Edgar Allen.*

For a moment, the two men stared at the cardboard poster of the young actress. Finally, Edgar said, "The movies blind people to the truth."

"And what's that?"

"That vampires are real."

The eyes in the shopkeeper's head seemed farther apart than usual, and his nose was crooked, perhaps broken in a fight many years ago. The result was disconcerting in that it made his left eye appear to be too far apart from its mate.

"Vampires aren't real," Murray said.

"That's what they want you to believe." Edgar's eyes flared with excitement. When they did so, the left eye seemed to drift off on its own. "Either that or they want to convince you that they're a bunch of farmers."

"Farmers?"

"Vampires that eat animals. That's fiction, man. Ain't no such thing. Vampires are about one thing—blood. *Human* blood."

Murray focused on the shopkeeper's right eye when he carefully asked, "So vampires control Hollywood?"

"How do you not know this?"

Edgar Allen was clearly a man prone to conspiracy theories. Murray could work with that if he were able to point him in the right direction. He'd have to be careful with how he asked his questions. "Have you heard about the attacks around town?"

The shopkeeper frowned and waved a dismissive hand. "That's not a bloodsucker." He returned to the counter. "That's a scam. Someone is pointing the cops in a different direction."

"You sound disappointed."

He shrugged before taking up his perch behind the counter.

Murray's eyes swept over the dusty artifacts lining the variety of shelves. There were all sorts of remnants from times gone past. There were books, toys, signs, and trinkets. There were empty product boxes and old military paraphernalia. Everything had the mustiness of time associated with them—not only from the era from which they came but from the length of time they had sat on these shelves.

He examined a boxed *Six Million Dollar Man* doll when he asked, "Is there money in the antique business?"

"Good enough."

Murray moved to another cabinet. "How long have you been at it?"

"You writing a book or something?"

"Just curious," Murray said.

"Be curious about buying something."

He bent over and looked down into a waist-high glass cabinet. There was a line of old

Timex watches. Murray glanced at the shopkeeper.

Edgar said, "Those are a good deal. They take a licking and keep on ticking. Don't find many like those today."

"You buy all these?"

"How else do you think I got 'em?"

Murray straightened. "People come in and sell stuff like this?"

When the shopkeeper didn't answer, Murray turned his head to look at him. He tapped the glass case.

"What's with the questions?" Edgar asked. "You a cop or something?"

"I'm looking for a watch."

"A Timex?" the shopkeeper asked.

"A Rolex."

Edgar's eyes slanted, and his jaw flexed. "I don't have any," he flatly said.

Murray's pulse quickened. "Has anyone come in trying to sell one today?"

"You think I'm a fence?"

"I didn't say that. I was only asking—"

"About stolen goods." The shopkeeper crossed his arms.

"You heard about Abner Dewey's watch?"

Edgar slowly nodded. "Word gets around."

"So someone came in and tried to sell a Rolex?"

"That's right, but I wasn't having any of it."

"Why not?"

"I know hot before I touch it, even before I heard about Abner's loss."

Murray walked over to the counter. "What did he look like?"

Edgar slowly shook his head. "I'm not a rat."

Hearing him utter those words stung. Murray's former self had turned rat against the Satan's Dawgs. FBI Agent Ekleberry coerced it, but he had informed, nonetheless. Even though he did it to protect the person he loved most in the world, he would forever be branded a rat and forced to live on the run from his former club.

"I heard he was big," Murray said.

"Could be."

"Nice suit and fancy shoes?"

"Same as everyone else on the island, I guess. Present company excluded."

Edgar didn't want to rat, but he was playing along with Murray's suggestions. He decided to continue to throw ideas out and see if he could get a better description.

"Glittery face?"

Edgar shrugged.

"Answer that one," Murray said. "It'll be the last one."

"Fine. No glitter."

Murray nodded as he thought. He recalled the man and woman he saw in the hotel lobby the previous evening. She glittered, and he didn't. Murray noticed it, but it didn't register as strange at that moment.

Something else tickled his memory. Murray closed his eyes to recall the scene. The two were in the lobby and snuggled together. The man had his arm around the woman. His suit was blue, and hers was maroon. He had a fancy watch. Murray wondered what kind it was.

The shopkeeper raised his eyebrows. "Remember something important?"

"Not sure. Maybe."

"Going to buy something?"

Murray rested an elbow on the counter. "Why didn't you call Chief Kern about the guy trying to pawn the watch?"

Edgar shrugged. "The chief and me, we don't get along."

"Why is that?"

"He's always in my business. Thinks the same thing you thought—that I deal in illegal goods. Which I don't."

"Then why not call Abner? Maybe earn yourself a reward."

The shopkeeper's lip curled. "Abner and Kern are friends. That alone dictates I can't help out the old coot."

"But you didn't buy the watch."

"I already said that. Listen, just because I won't deal in stolen property doesn't mean I've got to alert the cops or the aggrieved party. I figure I've done enough by not buying it. Let the chief do his job. And Abner should be more careful. Maybe he shouldn't talk so much."

Murray lowered his gaze as he thought about his next question.

Edgar leaned in to grab Murray's attention. "And if you aren't going to buy something, then shove off. You're taking up space for paying customers."

Murray glanced around the empty shop. Since he couldn't think of anything further to ask, he gave a short wave goodbye and headed toward the door. When his hand touched the doorknob, Edgar hollered, "Hey!"

He turned to face him.

"They're real, you know," the shopkeeper said.

"The vampires?"

The shopkeeper nodded. "Whether or not you believe in them, they believe in you."

"That sounds like something I heard in church as a kid."

Edgar Allen tapped his head. "Think for yourself. Even the devil tricked most of the world into believing he doesn't exist. You should believe in them before it's too late."

Chapter 13

Louise Welford sat behind the sales counter of Batty for Crafts. Her head was bent over an open book lain flat. Her finger trailed along with the words as she read. When Murray walked through the door, there wasn't an accompanying ding, so she didn't bother to look up or engage him in conversation.

He stopped just inside the entryway and examined the life-size cutout that stood nearby. It was of a menacing man in dark clothes. He had slicked-back hair, and his red eyes gleamed with intense fury. Near the corners of his thin, pale lips were sharp, white teeth.

Murray figured this must be the villain in the *Evenfall* movie, if not the series. The other cardboard characters did not seem threatening. This one, though, actually tried to be scary.

He shrugged and moved deeper into the store. Batty for Crafts catered to all sorts of hobbies. There were supplies for knitters and crocheters, of course, but the shop also carried the necessities for those who chose to draw, paint, scrapbook, or, well, there were so many things in the store that he couldn't figure out what they did.

Murray quickly found a basic set of needles, a skein of light brown yarn, and a small bag. He'd learned how to knit from his grandmother. It was a simple thing they shared whenever he came to visit. They often did it while they watched the reruns she preferred to modern television shows. He didn't mind the knitting or the old television shows because he loved being around Ma.

The act of knitting had become an outlet for him over the years. He'd often pull out his kit after he cleared the book on someone. Initially, the guys in the club thought his preferred way to reduce stress was a bit weird. Most of the crew had a method to deal with their mental tensions—drugs, women, or more violence were some of the things the other men deemed reasonable.

But Murray's old self was highly effective at what he did. Therefore, no other Dawg dared tease him.

As a bonus, many of the girls who hung around the club thought it was a sweet trait, and he often got extra attention because of it. One girl even asked him to teach her, and she ended up knitting a scarf for her mother. Beau, however, never completed any project. He would knit for a while, then pull out the stitches and rewrap the skein.

Those memories of knitting at the clubhouse percolated at the back of his mind while Murray selected his new kit. When he finished, he forced those old recollections away. He didn't want to spend too much time with his former self. That was a person he didn't like anymore.

As he approached the counter, the woman behind it looked up and smiled. "Come to see Louise today?"

Murray put his selected items on the countertop and frowned. He had thought this woman was Louise Welford, the owner of the store. She had been the woman at the restaurant. "Is Louise in?" he asked.

"I'm Louise," she said and tapped a nearby name tag that lay on the counter. It was the same official Belfry name tag the other store owners had worn.

"I'm Murray," he said.

"Welcome to Belfry, sweetie. They want us to wear these things," she said and tapped the tag once more. "But it makes Louise feel like an employee, and she didn't start a business to work for someone else."

Murray blinked several times as she beamed at him. Then she turned her attention to the items he selected. She flipped them over to find their prices. Then her fingers bounced across the register.

He said, "I heard someone robbed you last night."

Louise stopped ringing up his items and touched the bandage on her neck. "You heard about Louise's troubles, did you? Word gets around this little island something quick."

He nodded.

"It scared Louise something fierce." She glanced around before leaning in to whisper, "She almost wet herself; she was so scared."

Murray's nose crinkled. "You're Louise, right?"

She tapped the loose name tag again. "That's me. Miss Louise Welford. The one and only." Her hand settled on the cash register.

"What happened?" Murray asked.

She slowly crossed her arms. "Miss Louise already told the police..."

"Well—"

"And the girls at breakfast..."

"I'm helping—"

"But it won't hurt none to share the story again." A big smile creased her face. "Most people around here ignore Miss Louise, but you seem to be a nice young man, so she's happy to tell you." She pointed to the injury on her neck. "Louise didn't bite herself."

"That would be hard to do."

Louise Welford tapped the counter with a painted fingernail. "That's the point, young man. That's the point. What did you say your name was again?"

"Murray."

Her face brightened. "Really? Do you know that means 'lord and master'?"

"I didn't."

"It's a Gaelic name. Louise is of English descent and means 'famous warrior.' Don't you think it's fascinating? The origin of our names?" She held up the book she was reading. It was *The Origin of Baby Names* by Peter Vincent.

"You're reading *that*?"

"Why not? It's a suitable book with words and purpose. Why? What do you read?"

Murray didn't want to talk books with the older woman, especially since his inventory of books read was currently standing at one. So, he jerked his head toward the cardboard cutout at the front of the store. "Who's that?"

Her lips pursed as if she'd just eaten a lemon. "That's Kiefer. He's the leader of the Dreher House. They're the enemies of the Clan MacCrain."

Murray pointed to the book of baby names. "What does Kiefer mean?"

Her face brightened. "Miss Louise looked it up already. It means 'barrel maker.' Not nearly as strong as Murray or Louise, is it?"

Murray smiled. "Not even close."

"But Dreher means 'turner' as in someone who operates a lathe."

"Or turns a person into a vampire. Dreher doesn't seem like a baby name."

"It isn't. Miss Louise has all sorts of books on the origins of names. She's a little odd that way, looking up names and their origins."

She's odd in more ways than that, Murray thought.

Louise rubbed the bandage on her neck. "She almost forgot. You wanted the story of how this happened, didn't you?"

"If you don't mind."

"Well, yesterday was a particularly good day for the store."

Murray nodded politely.

"Lots of sales." Louise patted the top of the cash register.

"Visitors to the island freely spend whenever they're celebrating. That's why we have those silly greeters—" She pointed to the cardboard cutout. "And these." She tapped the name tag lying on the counter. "If it means more money in the cash drawer, Miss Louise is all for it."

The woman smiled brightly at Murray. An uncomfortable silence grew until she looked down at the goods spread across the counter, then the register. Louise looked at the rolled tape to confirm she rang up everything before announcing a total.

Murray pulled out a wad of bills and said, "You were telling me about last night's attack?"

"Oh, heavens. That's right. Age does funny things to the memory. Anyway, a good day for sales. That was said already, yes?"

He nodded.

"Well, Miss Louise went through the normal closing procedure. Lock the doors, add up the register, fill out a deposit slip, put the money and the slip into a bank bag. The normal process is to step out back, lock the rear door a final time, and deliver the deposit bag to the bank's night drop."

"Until someone interrupted you."

"That's what happened. *Exactly*. To the shock of Miss Louise, someone snuck up from behind and bit her on the neck. Right here." She called attention to the bandage she'd already been touching. "He snatched the money from her hand and ran off."

"Had you ever seen him before?"

She shook her head. "He grabbed Louise from behind. She never saw him."

"Did he say anything?"

Her eyes rolled up as she thought. Finally, she looked back at him and shook her head. "Not a word. He just bit Miss Louise and ran off. Stole almost twelve hundred dollars. What kind of person does that?"

"A vampire."

Her eyes drifted toward the cardboard cutout at the front of the store. "For all the good they've done this city, Miss Louise will never get used to those leeches. She's got a good mind to put Kiefer out on the sidewalk."

"I don't think Kiefer or any of the other cardboard cutouts bit you."

Louise smirked. "It does seem a bit farfetched to blame a barrel maker."

"It seems a person who would have robbed you would likely know your routine."

Louise's brow furrowed. "What are you saying? That it's someone who lives on the island?"

He looked to the rear of the store. "Mind if I look out back?"

"Are you a policeman or something? Miss Louise already told Chief Kern everything."

"I'm what some folks call a salvage consultant." Repeating the words gave him another thrill.

"Salvage consultant? What does that mean?"

"I suppose you have insurance."

"Miss Louise most certainly does, but it won't help her none in this matter. The deductible is fifteen hundred dollars. It doesn't make sense to pay that and still be out three hundred dollars. Miss Louise would be doing herself double the damage. She might be a bit touched." Louise winked. "But she still knows how to do simple math."

"What if I can find the money?"

"Do you think you can do that?"

Murray shrugged. "I don't know, but that's what a salvage consultant does. I find things people have lost."

"And when you do, you'll tell the chief where to find it?" Louise rubbed her hands together. "He'll arrest the man who robbed Miss Louise, and she'll get her money back?"

"That's assuming Kern can prove the money is yours."

The excitement faded from her face.

"No," Murray said, "what I'm thinking is this. I find your money and return it to you. And you'll be grateful and pay me a consulting fee."

"How much is this... *fee*?"

"Half."

"Half!"

"Right now, you've got zero. What I'm proposing, assuming I can locate your money, is you get half of what I recover."

Louise thought about it for a bit. "Well, there seems to be some logic in your argument."

"So, can I see where this robbery occurred?"

She nodded and led him to the rear of the store. He stepped out into the rain, but Louise stayed in the doorway as protection from the drizzle.

The alley proved to be nothing special. A row of single-story commercial buildings lined it. A small trash can was outside her door. On the opposite side of the alley was a little complex.

"What's that?" Murray asked.

"That's the Belfry assisted-living facility. Such sweet people live there."

To the right, he saw similar cans outside the other businesses lining the alley. Several doors down, he saw Shirley Herrick, the owner of the bookstore, dumping a small bag of trash into a can. She didn't notice him and stepped back inside.

To the left, at the end of the alley, across the street, stood a four-story building. Several windows on the second, third, and fourth floors had a view of where he stood.

"Is that the—"

"Boarding house," Louise said. "It is. Is that where you're staying?"

He nodded and stepped back inside. It was also where the man in the blue suit with the fancy wristwatch was staying.

"I should pay for my things and go," Murray said.

"Oh, that's right. You still have to pay Miss Louise." She patted her hands and hurried ahead to the counter.

He peeled off a couple of bills and handed them to her. After making change, she slipped his goods into a bag.

"Wish me luck," Murray said.

"Good luck," she said. When he neared the
door, Louise yelled, "And good hunting!"

Chapter 14

When Murray stepped into The Thirst of the Mind, his head was down. He really should have been more alert to his surroundings but being locked on the little island had lulled him into an odd sense of complacency.

Also, Abner Dewey's hijacked watch and Louise Welford's snatched money clouded his thoughts. The two chances to act as a salvage consultant were compounding his misplaced attention.

Due to this lack of focus, he again bumped into the cardboard cutout of Edmund MacCrain. Even though the wafer-thin vampire listed, his features remained serene.

Murray reacted quickly, though, and instinctively reached out to snatch the life-sized poster. Unfortunately, his diverted attention and jumbled thoughts caused him to misjudge the arc and speed of the fake vampire's fall.

Instead of rescuing the tumbling cutout, he smacked Edmund in the face. The slap of flesh against cardboard was surprisingly loud in the small bookstore.

In all fairness, the strike was wholly accidental and made with the back of an open hand. Be that as it may, the Edmund cutout was quite insubstantial compared to Murray's height and weight. The vampire had also very likely been portrayed by an actor who had never experienced a real fight. Not that the last supposition had any bearing on this exact moment, but it still seemed relevant to Murray for some reason.

All these thoughts, including the spiteful one about the actual actor, occurred in the briefest of moments—a flash, really—following the blow to Edmund's flat face.

Now, Murray hadn't seen the movies, and he didn't know the name of the man pretending to be a member of Clan MacCrain. For all he knew, the actor could have been a mixed martial arts champion. But from his mussed hair, glittery skin, pouty lower lip, and vacant stare, Murray could only surmise he'd never been punched in the face before.

Until now.

"Edmund!" Shirley cried from the far end of the store.

Murray bent to pick up the fallen vampire.

"Keep away!" she squealed.

He stopped with his hand around the cutout's neck. "It was—"

"Stand back," she gruffly ordered. She bent at the hips to rescue the fallen Edmund.

Murray lifted his hands and stepped away. "It was an accident."

Shirley glared up at him. "It wasn't an accident. I saw it. You attacked him."

"Attacked a piece of cardboard?"

"Are you okay, Edmund?" she whispered sweetly. She gently caressed the edges of the cutout as she assessed it for possible damage. "Did he hurt you?"

"I thought they were God's perfect creatures—that they couldn't be hurt."

She scowled and pointed an accusatory finger. "You!"

"I'm sorry," he said. "Really."

A young woman with long blond hair appeared at the back of the store and hurried toward the front.Underneath an unbuttoned sweater, she wore a T-shirt that read *I'm only here for the beer*. Her jeans were faded, but her red Converse shoes looked new. "What's going on?" she asked.

With her eyes still locked onto Murray, Shirley said, "He punched Edmund."

Murray shook his head. "It was an accident. I tried to catch him before he fell."

"He punched him!" Shirley said.

"It's okay, Mom." The younger woman reached out and touched Shirley on the shoulder. "Even I want to punch Edmund."

"Anna!"

Anna turned to Murray and apologetically said, "She's in love with Edmund."

"I am not," Shirley muttered as she embraced the cardboard cutout. "Too many people are bumping into him. I don't care what the Chamber says. He's not safe near the front." She moved deeper into the store with the life-size poster cradled in her arms. "He's staying behind the counter with me. Where it's safe."

Anna leaned in. "Like I said."

Murray watched the store owner step behind the counter with the cutout. She carefully wiped away unreal hairs that were not out of place.

Anna beamed at Murray. She was an attractive woman with the build of a professional volleyball player. He estimated her height at almost six feet.

"You're not here for the festival, are you?" she asked.

"No."

"I didn't think so," Anna said. "You don't seem the type."

"You don't seem too excited about it, either."

"Oh my God, I hate it."

"Then why are you in Belfry?"

She glanced back at her mom, who was distracted by Edmund's imagined needs. "I had a little trouble down in Odessa, so I thought I'd come to stay with my mom for a while."

"Trouble with the law?"

Anna's eyes took him in fully then, pausing at the tattoo on the back of his hand. "With an ex-husband," she said.

"Isn't there a song about all your exes living in Texas?"

She nodded.

"Belfry's gotta be a shock to the system."

"The goofiness, you mean?"

"And the weather."

"The weather doesn't bother me, but it's the fascination with the movies I don't understand. Some people get so into it, almost like a religion. They give up everything for the vampires and werewolves. It's make-believe and not even good make-believe, at that."

Murray lifted his chin toward Shirley. "Is that what your mom did when she moved here?"

Anna glanced back toward her mother. "She dropped everything to chase the dream. We were living in Midland when she told Dad she was leaving."

"Wow."

"What?"

"That's pretty intimate, don't you think?"

"Life's too short to beat around the bush," Anna said. "I believe in laying my cards on the table. What about you?"

Murray wasn't about to show her his cards, but he said, "I agree. Life is too short."

Anna watched her mother as she continued. "I was still a teenager when she left. She asked if I wanted to move with her. I didn't, of course, since I had my own life. Friends, school, you name it. All of it was more important than some stupid vampires that she loved. It didn't stop her, though. She bailed on us. Packed up to be near the heart of it all."

Shirley puttered behind the counter, chattering to Edmund as she went.

Anna's smile was soft. "She's nothing like the mother I remember."

"Better or worse?"

"Neither. She's sort of like a person on a spiritual quest, except she's searching for fictional vampires. Kind of silly, if you ask me."

"How'd your father take it?"

"After she'd gotten weird about the books and movies, he was glad she left. He never remarried, though. Just went about his life."

"And you?"

She shrugged. "I fell for the first man who promised to rescue me and take me away from it all. He slipped a ring on my finger when I turned eighteen, and we moved twenty miles up the road to Odessa. He promised we'd be together forever."

"What happened?"

"Life." For added measure, she shrugged and muttered, "Good times."

"Then you ended up here."

"In Vampire, USA. Did you come in just to punch Edmund in the face?" She lowered her voice. "Which is fine with me if that's the reason you did." Her voice returned to normal, "Or is there something I can help you find?"

"The second Travis McGee novel."

Her brow furrowed. "Travis McGee? I've never heard of him. What does he write?"

"He doesn't write anything. He's a detective written by John D. MacDonald."

"A mystery. She must carry it for the normals. It's probably in the back."

"It is," Murray said as he moved past her. "I've already seen it."

He walked toward the rear of the store and passed the glaring Shirley as he went. On the bottom shelf of the back wall, he found it—*Nightmare in Pink*. He slipped it out from the row of books, then stood to examine it.

"That's the one, huh?" Anna asked.

He nodded and handed her the book.

Rohan ambled out from an aisle to rub against Murray's leg. "I guess there won't be any lycans out tonight."

Anna looked down at the cat, then up to Murray. "You have got to be kidding me."

"Your mom told me about him."

She shook her head and said, "Don't encourage her." She handed the paperback back to Murray and walked toward the counter, where she proceeded to ring it up. Shirley stood by, her fingers absently caressing the edge of the Edmund cutout.

"Are you coming to the bonfire tonight?" Anna asked.

Murray handed her a couple of bills to cover the cost of the book. "I'm thinking about it."

"For someone who loves the movies as much as you—"

"I don't love the movies," Murray said.

"Uh-huh." Anna handed him back his change. "Well, if you come to the bonfire. I'll save you a spot."

Murray eyed her.

"I won't save him a spot," Shirley said. "He punched Edmund."

"Mom!" Anna hissed. "Give it a rest. Edmund had it coming."

Murray slipped the newly purchased paperback into his bag of knitting items and headed for the door.

"Goodbye," Anna called. "Hope to see you tonight!"

He waved goodbye before stepping outside.

Chapter 15

The rain had picked up while he was inside the store. He hunched his shoulders, lowered his head, and wished using an umbrella wasn't as uncool as it looked. While he walked up Main Street and watched several droplets cling desperately to the brim of his hat, Murray considered the various things he wanted to do back in his hotel room.

First, he would get out of his wet shoes and socks. He'd let them dry for a bit. Perhaps he should buy another pair, but his cash was limited. Unfortunately, Ted Onderdonk hadn't given him a credit card in the envelope. The marshal gave him one while he was in Maine and California, but perhaps there wasn't time when preparing the new identity. A thousand dollars was all Murray had to work with, so he needed to be careful. He'd already spent some of that on gas, food, and the hotel room.

He wasn't sure how much the repairs at Forge's would cost, let alone the hotel room, but his expenses were quickly mounting up. Murray didn't have many skills to refill his stash legally. He didn't want to resort to robbery, theft, or violence. Normal men didn't do that.

Therefore, the idea of acting as a salvage consultant was alluring. Finding Abner Dewey's watch and Louise Welford's money could be a windfall for him, both financially and emotionally. That extra consulting fee would help right his ship. Knowing he could earn money on his own—without the Satan's Dawgs or the U.S. Marshals—would help him believe he could fit in with the real world.

Thinking of Abner and Louise led him to the second thing he would do when he returned to the hotel. Could he do it in bare feet, though? Perhaps it should be the first thing he did. Regardless, he needed to talk with Sebastian, the front desk clerk, to ask the whereabouts of the man and woman who were in the lobby the previous night. The man was at the top of Murray's suspects. Actually, he was Murray's only suspect at this time.

But why do I suspect him?

Because his face didn't glitter.

He wore a big shiny watch.

He looked like a jerk.

Maybe it wasn't enough for a cop to work with, but it was enough for Murray. He turned at The Belfry Boarding House, bounded its steps, and stepped inside.

Almost immediately, Sebastian saw him, and the clerk's eyes widened. "Mr. Lee," he said and hurried from behind the counter.

"Hey, Seb—"

The attendant grabbed his arm. "Come with me."

Murray started to pull away, but Sebastian tugged insistently. "It's Chief Kern," he said. "You can't be here when he returns."

When he returns, Murray thought.

Sebastian pulled him toward the stairwell door and let it shut behind them.

"The chief was looking for you," the clerk said.

"I know. They searched my room this morning."

Sebastian shook his head. "No. He came back, but he was angry this time. He took your room key and went in."

"Without me there?"

The attendant nodded. "He said you weren't who you said you were. That I was supposed to watch out for you and call him when you showed up."

Murray eyed him. "Then why are you helping me?"

Sebastian smirked. "Kern's a bully. You're not the first guy he's done this type of thing to. You won't be the last. I've got no interest in helping him."

"Let me get this straight," Murray said. "He said I wasn't who I said I was?"

"That's right, and I'm supposed to call him or Colton when you return. Now, whatever you're doing is your business. I don't want to know."

Murray thought about the folded white envelope tucked into his back pocket. What if Kern found it? Would it prove anything? Maybe he should just destroy it now before he had a chance to study his history.

"Got someplace I can hide?" Murray asked. "Maybe another room?"

Sebastian's face took on an apologetic look. "We're booked. You got the last room because a guest didn't make it over before the bridge washed out."

Murray leaned his back against the wall. If there was ever a time to utter an expletive, it was now, but all he said was, "Crud."

The attendant watched him with an expectant look. He was waiting for Murray to provide him with some direction.

Well, if he couldn't get dry, he could at least get one of his questions answered. He pushed off the wall. "Last night, when I checked in, there was a man and a woman in the lobby."

Sebastian's brow furrowed. "You mean Charles Brewster?"

"The guy tangled up with a woman on the couch?"

He nodded. "Mr. Brewster has been with a different lady every night. He gets around."

"So, he's been here for some time?"

"Since the start of the festival. He's staying all the way through. All ten days."

"He came alone?"

Sebastian smirked. "He checked in alone, but he's never alone."

"What room is he in?"

"Four E. The top floor."

"Is he in now?"

"No, I don't believe so."

"Can you give me a key so I could look in his room?"

Sebastian shook his head.

"I'm sorry, Mr. Lee. I like you and all, but I can't do that. Helping you avoid Chief Kern is one thing, but letting you break into a guest's room..."

Murray patted the clerk's arm. "I get it. You've done enough. I appreciate it."

Sebastian leaned away to look through the small window of the stairwell door.

"One last thing," Murray said. "Which way does his room face?"

"What?"

"Brewster's room. Which way do the windows face?"

"Down Main Street," Sebastian said and pointed. "Although he's over the alley."

Murray was confused about his directions, so he asked another question. "Which direction is Batty for Crafts?"

The attendant's face pinched. "Really?"

Murray held up his bag of knitting supplies.

Sebastian's expression relaxed. "To each their own." He then pointed in the same direction he'd done a moment ago.

So, Murray thought, *lady's man Charles Brewster has a fourth-floor room with a view overlooking the alley where Louise Welford was robbed. He wears a fancy watch. And he looks like a big jerk.*

Murray was now sure he had his man.

Sebastian opened the stairwell door. "I've got to get back to the desk."

"Thank you," Murray said and followed him into the lobby.

The clerk returned to his perch behind the counter. "Be careful out there."

"I will."

Murray yanked the door to the boarding house opened. He quickly decided to buy some shoes and socks—he didn't want to get swamp foot while avoiding the cops—and stepped into the pouring rain.

In deference to the falling drops, he hunched his shoulders and bowed his head. He carefully descended the marble steps. Once on the sidewalk, he turned and bumped into someone large heading in his direction.

The brim of his baseball hat was forced down, temporarily blocking his vision.

Murray grunted in frustration, took a half-step back, and reset his hat. As he did so, his eyes focused on the smiling face of Chief Martin Kern.

"Just the guy I was looking for," Kern said.

"Chief."

The lawman reached out and patted Murray's shoulder. His smile was malicious when he asked, "How are you doing, Murray? Or can we cut the song and dance so I can call you Owen?"

Murray Lee blinked.

The chief's hand slid down to Murray's arm, and a vice grip tightened around his elbow. "I think we should go down to the station and have ourselves a little chat. What do you think about that, Mr. Hunter?"

Chapter 16

The Belfry Police Department was located five blocks away on First Street, one block north of Main. It was a small concrete block building divided into two portions. The west half housed the administrative wing while the east half contained several small jail cells. The entire operation was visible from the center of the structure.

Chief Kern escorted Murray the entire way to the station, as it was a short walk. They hadn't bothered to talk during this time, and Kern let go of Murray's elbow after he didn't attempt to pull free.

Why bother? Where would he go with both bridges still out of commission?

Patrons in various stores hurried to the windows to observe the perp walk the chief had Murray on. It wasn't the first time he had been paraded in front of citizens by a law enforcement officer, but Murray hadn't expected it ever to occur again.

As they passed through downtown, glittery vampires no longer bothered to act disaffected. Instead, they stood under their umbrellas and watched with interest as the two men strode along the sidewalk.

Several Belfry citizens walked in the opposite direction. As they passed the two men, they respectively muttered either "Chief" or

"Martin," even as they eyed Murray with suspicion or disdain.

As they neared Batty for Crafts, Louise Welford blinked several times from behind her store window. She waved slightly at them. Both men nodded politely back.

At the pharmacy, Pam Benson crossed her arms and slowly shook her head.

Shirley and Anna Herrick watched from the storefront of The Thirst of the Mind. Flat Edmund stood in the middle of the two with Shirley's arm tightly around the cutout's waist. Concern registered in Anna's eyes.

By the time they made it to The Lost Toys, it seemed as if the entire town knew Murray was being led around by Chief Kern. Hidden in the darkened corner of a window display, Edgar Allen watched the two men with great interest. He appeared to be a shabbily dressed gargoyle, desperately trying to get lost in the shadows.

But the chief noticed the leering antique store owner and glowered at him. The sudden attention from Kern startled Edgar. Embarrassed to have been caught ogling them, Edgar stumbled out of the display, knocking over items as he went.

When they were inside the chief's office, Kern took off his coat to hang it on a wall hanger. He tilted his baseball cap up on the back of his head. It was an attempt to make him look relaxed, perhaps non-threatening. Murray had seen it before. All it did was make Kern look like a down-on-his-luck hick.

Murray pulled his baseball hat down tighter around his eyes.

"Some coffee?" Kern asked.

He slowly shook his head.

"No need to be tough, Owen."

"I'm not trying to be tough, *Martin*."

"That's Chief Kern to you," he said. "Only my friends get to call me Martin."

Murray shrugged.

"And we're just having a conversation," Kern added.

"So, I'm not under arrest?" He started to stand. "I'm free to go?"

Kern waved away the questions and pointed to the chair where Murray had been sitting. "You knew you weren't under arrest several blocks ago, yet you still came all this way. You want to know what I know."

Murray dropped back into the chair. "I came with you because you're the law, *Martin*."

The chief's face flattened.

Murray raised his eyebrows. If the chief expected an apology, he would be waiting for some time.

Eventually, Kern scrunched his nose and looked in the air. A moment later, he shrugged and said, "I called Ace Adventures."

Murray stiffened.

Kern shifted in his chair. "When I asked for Owen Hunter, it turned into a game of twenty questions with the operator. Who was I? Why was I asking about him? How did I know Owen? Got so I felt like I was the one in trouble."

"Maybe it was a nosy operator."

The chief raised an eyebrow. "Maybe. She put me on hold for a while. When she came back, she said Owen was out for the day, but she'd let him know I called."

Murray relaxed. That was a better response from the marshals than he had expected.

"It felt like she was covering for someone," Kern said. "This isn't my first rodeo. I know when someone's yanking my chain."

"When Owen calls you back," Murray said, "this whole thing will be settled."

"It's already settled," Kern said. A self-satisfied smile spread across his lips. "Guess who else I talked to?"

He had a pretty good idea but didn't want to say.

"Come on, Owen. Don't be that way."

Hearing the other name again, Murray crossed his arms. The lawman wanted to play a game, so Murray needed to settle in for it.

"Detective Roy Cochran says hi."

Murray's face remained passive, but he could feel his pulse quicken. Roy Cochran was the detective who initially suspected him of murder in Costa Buena, California. Well, he actually suspected Owen Hunter, but Owen was Murray. Or actually, Murray was Owen.

Yeah, Murray thought, *that's the better way to think of it.*

"Not going to admit to anything, huh?" Chief Martin Kern asked.

Murray lifted his eyebrows.

"Not going to deny that you're Owen Hunter?"

Deny the accusation or lean into it? he wondered. He sucked in his lips, then lowered his eyes.

"Before you even think about denying it," Kern said, "let me tell you some things." The chief lifted a finger. "First, your vitals match. Owen's and Murray's match perfectly. I checked both of you through California DMV. Your birth dates are different, and your criminal records are different. I haven't quite figured that part out, but the vitals are exact. Height, weight, hair color, eye color."

"Lot of people can be my size—"

"Hardly," the chief said. Then he raised two fingers. "And second, Detective Cochran mentioned your tattoos. That one on your right hand—" Kern's eyes flicked to the inky ball of fire. "It's sort of hard to hide."

"A lot of people have this tattoo," Murray said.

"On the back of the right hand? Don't try to defend it, because he described others that go up and down your arms. How about you take off that jacket and let me see if his descriptions match?"

Murray's jaw flexed.

"So I'm right," Kern said with a smile. "The only thing that doesn't match is how complimentary Cochran was of you. He blathered on and on about how decent a guy Owen Hunter was. When I asked about Murray Lee, do you know what he said?"

"No, Martin, I don't."

The chief's lip twitched. "That's chief. You're messing with me, and I know it. Best knock it off, *Owen*. Detective Cochran said, and I bet you already know this, he said he'd never heard of a Murray Lee."

Murray remained silent and tried unsuccessfully to slow his heartbeat.

"I poked at his memory a couple of times. I asked if Murray and Owen might have hung out together. No, he said. He was adamant about it. He told me that Owen was a loner. Just like you."

He watched the chief nod with satisfaction. The lawman was enjoying this moment.

"A funny thing happened when I mentioned Murray Lee's description exactly matched Owen Hunter's. Guess what that was."

Murray opened his mouth, but Kern snapped his fingers and pointed at him.

"Don't bother, because I'll tell you. Detective Roy Cochran clammed up so quickly it surprised me. He stopped offering anything except how sweet of a guy Owen was. He said it so much I wanted to stick my finger down my throat and barf." Kern mimed as much.

At that moment, Murray's pulse suddenly slowed. He wasn't in trouble, and he knew what this was. It was typical law enforcement fishing. It might have been a little politer than what he was used to while he was a member of the Satan's Dawgs, but Kern was simply looking for wrongdoing. And Murray hadn't done anything wrong.

"What have you got on Roy Cochran?" Kern asked.

"Excuse me?"

"What are you hanging over the detective's head? Got some blackmail?"

"I don't have anything on him," Murray said.

"You must. Otherwise, I don't understand why a guy like him would clam up so quick. Doesn't make sense unless you got him over a barrel."

Murray shrugged.

"Can you see the problem I've got? Owen Hunter and Murray Lee. Two loners with identical attributes and identical tattoos, but different birthdays and different criminal histories. There may not be a crime in there, but it's got me intrigued."

Kern leaned forward and put his elbows on his desk. He steepled his fingers and studied Murray. The two men stayed silent for some time. Finally, Kern asked, "Why'd you visit with Abner Dewey?"

Even though Murray didn't want a lawman interested in himself or his background, he couldn't help himself when he crossed his legs and said, "It's like this, Martin."

"I told you—"

He lifted his hand to cut off Kern. "I know. Only your friends get to call you Martin."

The chief's face reddened, which pleased Murray. He knew this violated one of Marshal Onderdonk's principles—*Do not develop habits from your old life*—but tweaking an officer, especially the chief of police, was a rare opportunity he couldn't pass up.

"I wanted to hear about Abner's bite," Murray said.

"Why would you care? You didn't know the man."

"It seemed... interesting."

The chief fell back into his chair. "Well? Did he tell you anything?"

"Only that he got bit, and someone stole his watch."

Kern scratched the side of his face. "I also heard you talked with Miss Louise."

Murray pointed to his bag of knitting supplies. "I needed a kit."

The chief rifled through the plastic sack and frowned. "You're kidding."

"It's a stress reliever."

"What's this?" he said and held up the McGee adventure. "*Nightmare in Pink*? Sounds like a dirty book."

"It's a mystery."

Kern looked over the top of the paperback. "You read?"

"What are you saying?"

"I'm saying you don't look much like a reader."

"What's a reader supposed to look like?"

"Not you," the chief said and shoved the book back in the sack.

"I do something to make you mad, Martin?"

"*Chief*," he sternly said and crossed his arms. "I don't understand the two names, and that bothers me, especially since you haven't explained your part in it."

"In what?"

"In the whole convoluted mess. The similarities between you two. Owen and Murray. Murray and Owen."

"But is that a crime?"

The chief rubbed his hand over his chin. "I don't know yet. There might be one in there, and I haven't found it yet. But if there is, I'll find it. Believe you me."

"That can't be the only thing that's made you mad," Murray said.

The chief leaned forward again. "How about this? I don't trust you."

"What did I do?"

Kern slapped his desk. "Mister, I can't figure you out."

"Again, I ask. Is that a crime?"

The chief pointed at him. "Don't be cute. You aren't one of those slick mainlanders with their bloodsucker fantasies. If you were one of them, I could relax. Whenever the festival is going on, something weird, maybe kinky, happens. At least, I know what I'm dealing with when those types are around. But you? I don't know what you're here for, and that irks me."

"I made a wrong turn onto the island. Ask anyone, Martin."

Kern's face twisted. "*Chief.* For the last time, it's chief, and nobody makes a wrong turn onto Belfry. It's impossible."

"I did."

The radio on the chief's desk squawked then. *"Hey, Chief?"*

Kern kept his eyes on Murray as his hand reached for the microphone. He squeezed the button as he spoke. "Yeah, Colton?"

"You know those bikers you wanted me to keep an eye on?"

"What about them?"

"Half of them took off in a real hurry."

The chief's brow furrowed, and he turned his attention to the microphone. "Where'd they go?"

"I don't know. They just jumped on their bikes and rode away."

Kern thought for a moment. When he looked up, his eyes caught Murray's. He squeezed the microphone's transmit button again. *"Thanks for the update, Colton."* The chief jerked his head toward the receiver and asked Murray, "You know anything about that?"

"About a microphone? Yeah, sure. You squeeze the button and talk. Someone on the opposite end does the same thing, and, voila, you have a conversation."

"Smart."

"I'm no dummy."

The chief studied him for a moment before asking. "The guys on the other side of the river. They want to get into town real bad."

Murray shrugged. "Maybe they're fans of *Evenfall.*"

"You think that, do you?"

"I don't know," he said. "What's not to love about sparkly vampires and bare-chested werewolves?"

The chief's frown twisted into a smirk.

Murray stood. "I assume I'm free to go."

Kern opened his hands in a what-can-I-do gesture before standing behind his desk.

The two walked to the front door, with the chief dutifully following behind. Murray stopped, turned to the lawman, and let a slow, mischievous smile spread across his lips.

Kern's face purpled in anticipation.

"Thanks for the conversation... *Martin.*"

"Chief!"

"Gesundheit."

As Kern's eyes narrowed, Murray chuckled and pushed open the door.

Chapter 17

The rain was more than a drizzle as Murray headed back up Main Street. No one paid much attention to him since Chief Kern no longer escorted him.

Sharply dressed vampires walked under their umbrellas with elongated strides and exaggerated hip thrusts. Whenever he neared them, they paused and affected the look of a statue. Only their eyes trailed him as he passed by.

He had no idea what the purpose of this was, but he took to pausing near these visitors now, freezing them for extended periods in their statue-like poses.

A man sharply dressed in a tailor-cut suit with pointy shoes and a handkerchief inserted in a breast pocket halted as Murray neared. He thrust out his hip and cocked his umbrella over a shoulder. He placed a manicured hand on his waist and flattened his facial features.

As soon as this pretend vampire froze into position, Murray stopped walking and moved underneath his umbrella. He took his time looking up and down Main Street, enjoying the protection provided from the rain.

Earlier, Murray had decided carrying an umbrella was most uncool. Now, he decided hijacking someone else's umbrella may be one of the most fun things he could do while in Belfry.

"C'mon, man," the visitor mumbled through closed lips.

Murray turned to face the fake vampire. "You say something?"

The visitor's eyes casually drifted away, but he remained frozen in position.

From his sack of goodies, Murray pulled out his paperback. He opened it and said, "Chapter one." He turned to the visitor. "I should probably ask if you like mysteries, but you wouldn't answer me, would you? Since it doesn't matter, let's give it a read." Murray started the second Travis McGee novel. "She worked in one of those Park Avenue buildings—"

The vampire clucked his tongue. "Really?"

"What?"

"Normals." The pretend vampire uttered it as if it were a curse word before angrily stalking away.

Murray chuckled and slipped his book back into the sack.

He played the stop-and-bother-the-fake-vampires game all the way back to the boarding house. Word must have gotten around quickly because the last couple he approached hurried by him without pausing to affect a look of casual disregard.

That made him happy.

Murray bounded the stairs to the boarding house and entered.

Now, he was back in his room and barefoot. His wet shoes and socks were sitting on top of the radiator. Since he didn't buy replacements for either, he had to wait for them to dry. He wondered how long that would take.

He sat on the bed and scooched until his back rested against the headboard. For a while, he studied the history of Murray Lee. It was, as Waylon Forge suggested, rather dull.

As a cover, he had never caused too much trouble, and he'd never done anything exciting. Whether it was interesting didn't matter, he decided. He still needed to commit it to memory. After a few minutes, though, he tired of studying and set the document aside.

He grabbed the phone from the nightstand and dialed a number.

"Ace Adventures," a woman smoothly said, "where your journey begins. How may I help you?"

"This is Murray Lee. I'd like to talk with Mr. Onderdonk about my reservation."

From the other end of the line, he heard clicking on a keyboard. "Mr. Lee. Ah, yes, I see you right here." More clicking. "Huh. We don't have you reserved anywhere."

"That's my problem. My last reservation—"

"Please hold," she said, and the line went silent.

He rubbed his feet together. They were still cold after walking in the rain. He alternated which foot was on top for a bit, but realized it wasn't helping much, especially the toes. He crossed his legs by bringing his feet under his thighs. He then rubbed the toes with his free hand.

When the operator came back on the line, she said, "Mr. Lee? We're sending a representative out to speak with you."

"What about Onderdonk?"

"He's unavailable at this time."

"What's that mean?"

"Sir, we're sending some—"

"No," he said. "Tell me what's going on, or I'm done. This is unaccept—"

"Hold, please."

"Wait—"

The phone went silent again. He stared at the phone receiver. They had traced the call. That was obvious, since the operator said they were sending another marshal out to him. However, knowing where he was wouldn't do them any more good than it was doing the Satan's Dawgs. The bridges being out gave him a little breathing room from everybody who wanted to keep track of him.

Maybe he should make a break for it once the bridge reopened. Could he drop off the radar and just disappear? Vanishing was harder than most people thought. It required a lot of help.

He had it when he vanished as Beauregard Smith, only to reappear in Pleasant Valley under a different identity. Could he do it this time without the help of the U.S. Government?

Would I want to?

The government helped get him into this mess.

Murray sighed.

No, he reminded himself. He was the one who got himself into this life. No one else made these decisions for him. Accepting responsibility for his choices was the first step in changing his life. He wanted to blame others, but doing so would pull him back into the habits of his old life.

"Mr. Lee?" A man's voice pulled him from his thoughts.

"Yes."

"I regret to inform you that Marshal Onderdonk was shot."

"Shot! Is he all right?"

"He's recovering, but he's under sedation."

Costa Buena, Murray thought. One or more of the Dawgs must have shot him when he stayed behind to slow them down.

"And Ekleberry?"

"His Blackberry? We recovered it. Luckily, no operational security was compromised."

"Ekleberry," Murray repeated. His tone revealed his frustration. "FBI Agent Max Ekleberry. What about him?"

The man mumbled something he couldn't hear. There was tapping on the keyboard. "We don't show any record of a Max Ekleberry."

"Don't you people talk to each other? I already asked your other operator this."

"Sir, we're doing the best we can. I'll reach out to our sister agency to get an update on their agent."

"I'd appreciate that."

Murray rubbed his cold feet together.

"Sir, are you currently in trouble with the law?"

He stopped rubbing his feet. "Why do you ask?"

"We received a call from a Chief Kern of the Belfry Police Department. He was inquiring about your... ahem, a former acquaintance of yours."

"Everything is fine," Murray said. "I've got it under control."

"That's good to hear," the man on the line said. He sounded like a high school math teacher. "As a reminder, Mr. Lee, this phone number is not to be shared with people who aren't on your account."

Murray mumbled. "I understand."

"Can I reach you again at the number you're calling from?"

"Yeah, sure."

"Stay near this number until a new customer service representative arrives to help you."

"They won't be able to get to me."

The man on the other end of the line chuckled. "We're Ace Adventures, Mr. Lee. We can get to anyone."

Chapter 18

He padded up the staircase in his bare feet, pushed a windowed door open to the fourth floor, and peered into the hallway. Not seeing anyone, Murray stepped out.

There wasn't a sign indicating which direction room 4E was, so he started to his right, then stopped as he saw signs indicating rooms C and B.

He spun around and headed in the opposite direction. Pausing outside room 4E, he listened for several minutes but didn't hear anything. He reached for the doorknob, irrationally hoping it would be unlocked, and tried to open the door.

It was secure.

For a moment, he considered entry by brute force.

What would that get him?

First, he was barefoot. Kicking the door would hurt. And if he did get entry, he'd have a lot more trouble than he wanted.

The inhabitant of the room, Charles Brewster, would know someone had gained illegal entry and the hotel would call the police.

A brute force entry did not seem like a smart choice.

He wasn't about to give up, though.

Murray walked the entire floor and didn't find what he wanted. More than likely, it was on the first, but he now had time on his side so he could afford to be patient. He walked down to the third floor and repeated the process.

He walked the entire level but didn't locate what he was after. He stepped into his room, however, and checked on how his shoes and socks were doing on the radiator. They were still wet.

Murray ruefully shook his head. He'd only been gone for a few minutes. What did he expect would happen? That they would dry quicker with him gone?

After leaving his room, he entered the stairwell and dropped to the second floor. Again, he didn't find what he wanted.

So that left the first floor, which meant the possibility of prying eyes, especially the desk clerk, Sebastian. At the stairwell door leading to the lobby, Murray paused. He stared through the little window and noticed a large group of glittering men and women standing about. They were smiling and laughing.

Murray stepped into the lobby and moved toward the end of the hallway. He soon found what he was searching for—a maintenance closet.

He reasoned there should be a set of keys or, at the very least, a master key, inside for a janitor to use. He fought back a smile, grabbed the door handle, and turned.

It was locked, and his grin faded.

Murray glanced toward the front of the lobby, and the crowd of shimmering and chattering vampires began to thin. It appeared they were leaving the hotel.

Charles Brewster's room was locked.

The maintenance closet was secured.

And the only key he knew of was behind the desk with Sebastian.

It was time he tried to convince the hotel clerk to give him the key. The man had already turned him down once, though. He wasn't sure what he would do differently this time.

As he turned the corner into the lobby, Murray halted.

Standing before him, in all his non-glittering glory, was Charles Brewster. On his arm was an alluring redhead in a slinky green dress. The left side of her face sparkled under the hotel lights.

Brewster stood slightly taller than Murray. The man's eyes traveled Murray's length. "You should remove your shirt," he said.

Murray's face warmed. "Excuse me?"

"If you want to be one of the lycans, I mean. Otherwise, running around barefoot makes you look destitute."

The redhead giggled. "Oh! Do it. Take off your shirt. No one is playing as a lycan."

Murray frowned.

"Please, Charlie," the woman pleaded. "Make him do it."

Brewster cocked his head toward his playmate. "Do it for the girl."

Murray frowned. "That's not what I'm here for."

"Aww," the woman whined.

The joy faded from Brewster's face. "What's your story then?"

"No story. My shoes are wet, and I came downstairs to see Sebastian." His eyes flicked to the man behind the counter.

The desk clerk eyed him with curiosity.

"No story?" Brewster said. He squeezed the woman's waist. "That's new."

She giggled. "No story, and he's barefoot?"

"Don't let us keep you," Brewster said. He spun around, almost lifting the woman as he did so. She giggled with the movement. Once outside, he opened an umbrella and held it over them. They moseyed down the stairs and disappeared around the corner.

Murray turned to Sebastian. "Do you know where they're going?"

"Dinner, I suppose."

"So he'll be out for a while?"

The desk clerk shrugged. "A couple of hours, I would guess."

Murray hurried to the counter and whispered, "I need the key to his room."

Sebastian frowned. "I can't do that."

He reached into his pocket and pulled out his wad of bills. "How much will it take—"

"Why do you want into his room?"

"I think he's behind the attacks on Abner Dewey and Louise Welford."

Sebastian glanced around before leaning in. "Charlie? It doesn't make any sense."

"Yeah, it does, but it'll take too long to explain."

The attendant pulled back. "You *really* believe it's him?"

Something in Sebastian's eyes glinted with excitement. He wouldn't give the key to Murray, but perhaps he might use the key in his aid.

"Want to help me solve the case?" Murray asked.

The clerk's face brightened. He quickly turned to a keyboard behind the counter and grabbed the key to room 4E. When he faced Murray again, he whispered, "Nobody can know about this."

Chapter 19

The room was clean and orderly. The bed was expertly made. Nothing was on the counters. It almost appeared vacant.

"Strange," Sebastian whispered.

"What is?" Murray asked.

"He's got a Do Not Disturb sign on the door. We haven't cleaned the room for several days. This looks as clean, maybe cleaner than when he first checked in."

"So he's cleaning his room? Making his bed?"

"Or not staying here," the attendant muttered.

Murray began moving around the room, but Sebastian stood near the door.

"You going to help?" Murray asked.

Sebastian lifted his hands. "This is your deal." He swung the key around his index finger. "I already did my part."

Murray frowned but moved toward the dresser. He didn't have time to get in a back and forth with the desk clerk.

First, he pulled open the bottom drawer. Inside were several pairs of nicely folded pants. In the middle drawer were carefully folded underwear and balled socks. The top drawer held three watches, belts, and loose change.

He examined each watch in turn. There was a black Blancpain, a gold Tudor, and a silver Rolex. He lifted the final timepiece to show

Sebastian. "Abner had a Rolex stolen. What do you want to bet this is it?"

"You think?"

Murray slipped the watch into his pocket.

"You can't take that," Sebastian whispered.

"Why not?"

The clerk glanced around the small room. "It's stealing."

"It was already stolen."

"How do you know?"

"I know."

Sebastian looked around the room again. "He'll know it's gone."

"What do I care?" Murray said. "We'll have caught him, and the chief can arrest him."

Sebastian shook his head. "I don't like this."

"Trust me."

"I don't even know you."

"We're catching a thief."

"By acting like thieves?" Sebastian put his hands to his head. It was apparent that this had become too much for the man to bear.

Murray moved to the closet and opened the bi-fold doors. He rifled through the pockets of the hanging jackets. When his hands wrapped around something thick and heavy, he smiled at Sebastian.

"What?" the clerk asked. "What did you find?"

From the inner pocket of a suit jacket, Murray tugged out a small canvas bag with the logo of Batty for Crafts. It was the size of a container used for pencils or other small supplies.

Murray unzipped the bag to expose many bills of various denominations. "Wanna bet that this was Miss Louise's deposit?"

Sebastian's eyes widened. "That dirty dog," he said. He no longer bothered with whispering.

Murray tucked the small canvass bag into his back pocket. "Let's go," he said. "It's time to catch our thief."

Chapter 20

On a beach at the northeast corner of the island, the citizens of the town built an elaborate bonfire. Even a drizzle couldn't put a damper on this celebration.

Murray had been to these types of things before. Usually, they were hastily assembled events. When he was younger, his friends would gather some wood, spray lighter fluid on it, and stand around awkwardly as they drank stolen beer.

If he had to give the Satan's Dawgs credit for one thing, it was that they knew how to throw a party. Their bonfires tended to be sprawling celebrations of lawlessness. The fires at the center of them would sometimes be a raging affair, while at others, it might not be much more than something to roast marshmallows over. Regardless, the frivolity around the flames was something he never expected to surpass.

Until this moment on the small island of Belfry, Oregon.

The residents built a giant monument to the movie gods who brought them *Evenfall.* Perhaps some of the locals hated the films, maybe even most of them did, but as flames licked the heavens, the citizens of Belfry danced in circles and thrust red plastic cups toward the stars.

Classic rock music played from a white van that had its rear doors open. Right now, Warren Zevon's "Werewolves of London" blasted through the speakers.

Before coming to the bonfire, Murray had attempted to contact Abner Dewey at his home and Louise Welford at her shop. He struck out both times. Now, seeing the size of the party at the bonfire, he imagined that they both were here.

As Murray approached the fire, Waylon Forge wandered over with the three-legged Wrecker at his side. The older man wore a rain jacket with the hood lifted over his beanie-covered head. Forge raised a plastic cup in salute. "Mr. Lee," he said with a lopsided grin.

"No *Dancing with the Stars* tonight?"

"On bonfire night? Are you crazy? Even *The Bachelor* could be on, and the Mishes would skip it." He searched the nearby revelers. "She's around here shomewhere if you'd like to meet her."

Murray pulled back slightly, as he could smell the alcohol on Forge's breath. In his former life, a drunken man slurring his words would have been part of everyday life. But now, he wished he could slip away. However, he needed some information from Forge, so he had to stay engaged in this conversation for just a few moments longer.

"How are the repairs coming?" Murray asked.

Forge frowned. "Shame ash before." He sipped greedily from his cup. "Shtill ain't got da part."

Wrecker hopped over to Murray, and the big man petted the wet dog.

"Enjoying the feshtival?" Forge asked.

"Making do."

Forge's smile was crooked as he chuckled. "That's da feshtival shpirit."

Edgar Allen ambled over. "Waylon," he said, "isn't it past your bedtime?"

Forge saluted with his cup again. "To you, Edgar. May your vampires be forever preshent." Then he attempted a sip. His brow furrowed, and he turned the cup over. He shook it several times and looked inside it. Then the older man looked at his dog. "Lesh go, boy. Lesh go find mawmaw since pawpaw needs another drink."

They watched the older man and his dog wander off. When the two were out of earshot, Edgar said, "Saw you had some trouble with the law today."

"Kern had some questions for me."

"Looked more serious than that."

"It wasn't." Murray eyed Edgar. "The chief doesn't like you. That was clear."

Edgar shrugged. "No one believes in vampires."

Murray stared at him.

"What about you?" Edgar asked.

He wasn't sure what to say, so to get along with the wild-eyed man, so he said, "I still believe."

"Still?"

"When I was a kid, I saw a vampire movie. It made me want to believe in them."

"Which one?" Edgar asked, as his face brightened with excitement. "*Dracula? Nosferatu? Isle of the Dead?*"

"The one with Lauren Hutton as a vampire countess."

Edgar frowned and waved him off dismissively. "Ah, you don't believe."

"I believed in Lauren Hutton. She was quite something."

The shop owner's displeasure turned into a scowl. He turned and ambled away.

Murray moved closer to the towering bonfire. The heat radiating off it warmed him. Nearby, he noticed Abner Dewey standing alone and staring into the blaze.

He hurried to him.

"Abner."

"Hmm?"

"I've got something to show you." Murray reached into his pocket and removed the watch he'd taken from Charles Brewster's room. He cupped the silver timepiece in his hand to show it discreetly to the older man.

"What's that?" Abner asked.

Perhaps Abner had poor eyesight. Murray lifted it higher and turned it so the bonfire would illuminate it better.

The older man cocked his head. "What do I want with that?"

Suddenly unsure of himself, Murray said, "It's your father's Rolex."

Abner cocked his head. "That is most definitely not my father's. His was dinged up. It had a leather band. It was a watch that experienced life. That watch—" Abner leaned forward to examine the timepiece that Murray held in his hand. "Looks like the watch of a fancy pants. It's pristine. Nary a scratch."

Murray wrapped his fist around the timepiece.

"I thought you said you were a salvage expert," Abner said.

"*Consultant*," Murray said. "I'm a salvage consultant."

"Well, if that doesn't explain nothing." The older man turned and walked off.

Murray shoved the watch into his pocket. Worry entered his mind now. Had he'd stolen the Rolex of an honest man?

But there was still the bag of cash with the Batty for Crafts logo in his pocket.

He hurried through the crowd, looking for Louise Welford. Not finding her, he paused and put his hands on his hips.

"What do you think?" a woman asked. Murray turned to find Anna Herrick staring at him with wide, hopeful eyes. "It's wonderful, don't you think?"

"What is?"

"The fire." Her arms swept toward the giant ball of orange like Vanna White announcing a winning phrase on *Wheel of Fortune*. "I saw it a couple years ago when I visited my mom, and it blew me away."

Several feet behind Anna stood her mother, Shirley. Her hands fiddled with the drawstrings of her rain jacket. Mother Herrick looked slightly uncomfortable away from her bookstore and the watchful leer of Flat Edmund.

Murray's eyes shifted to the fire. "It's big."

"Big?" Anna laughed. "That's all you can say? This fire could alert an aircraft. It's so big they probably could see it from the moon."

"It's not that big," he muttered as he searched the crowd again for Miss Louise.

"You're a hard man to impress." Anna touched his arm. "What are you doing after?"

"After?"

"After the bonfire."

"Going back to my room," he said. Realizing he might have just said the wrong thing, he added, "to read."

"Read?"

"The book I bought."

"I know," she said with a nervous laugh. "But I thought maybe you would like, you know, to get a drink or something. Or maybe you would like some company?"

"No, thanks," Murray said.

Anna blinked several times.

"There's a girl," he explained.

"Here?" Anna asked, glancing around.

"No."

Anna's gaze returned to him. "Oh. You love her?"

Murray shrugged. He didn't know if it was love, but it was definitely something.

"Huh," Anna said. She lifted her red cup and wandered off.

Shirley Herrick followed her daughter without a word to Murray.

Again, he searched the crowd for Louise Welford. He thought he caught a glimpse of her and headed that direction. But she wasn't where he expected her to be, and he stopped. He paused to search the crowd again.

When another woman said, "I didn't think you would show," Murray casually turned to see Georgia from the Belfry Bruncheonette smiling at him. "Who are you looking for?"

He stood on his tiptoes to get a better view. "Louise Welford," he muttered.

"What for?"

"To say hi."

"The old gal certainly made an impression on you."

Murray dropped back to his normal height and faced her.

"That's better," Georgia said, looking up at him. "How are you enjoying Belfry?"

He started to answer, but she said, "Oh, jeez, that was a stupid question. I'm sorry for asking that. You're not here for the festival, are you? It's been a long time since I've done this."

"This?"

"Talk with a man."

"We talked this morning."

"I took your order."

"Oh."

She sipped from her red cup. "Listen," she said, then glanced around. "You want to go somewhere, maybe? Get a drink? Or talk?"

"I'm sorry," he said.

"Sorry?"

"There's a girl," Murray said.

"A girl? Here?" The way she said it made it sound like she was jealous of someone.

"No. She's back east."

"And she's your girlfriend?"

He nodded. What would it hurt to say Daphne Winterbourne was his girlfriend?

"I don't want to get in the way of love, I guess." Georgia frowned. "But if you change your mind, I'll be around."

She drifted off toward another part of the crowd.

Murray finally saw Louise Welford and started toward her, but a hand reached out and grabbed his arm.

"If it isn't my good buddy, Owen Hunter," Chief Kern said. "Staying out of trouble?"

Murray thought about the possibly stolen watch in his pocket. "Doing my best."

Kern's radio squawked on his hip. He removed it and lifted it to his ear. "Go ahead, Colton."

"Hey, Chief, we got a report that there's a small boat coming across the Columbia."

"With as rough as it is?"

"That's what they're saying. The report is they've got no running lights."

"What are they using for a guide?" Kern's voice trailed off as he stared at the roaring bonfire. "See if you can spot them. Darn fools are probably going to get themselves killed trying to cross at night. I'll head toward the river's edge now."

"Will do, Chief."

"People do that often?" Murray asked. "Try to cross the river?"

"Not the smart ones," Kern muttered as he clipped his radio to his belt.

Murray stared into the darkness. For a second, he wondered who would be foolish enough to cross the Columbia River under cover of darkness. He knew only one group who would attempt such a dangerous thing—the Satan's Dawgs.

Kern studied Murray. "You remember our deal, Owen. As soon as the bridge is open, you're off this island."

"You won't have to escort me," Murray said. "I can promise that much."

"Excuse me, Chief."

Both men turned to see Charles Brewster and the redhead he held around the waist. Murray's heart raced.

"Charlie," the chief said with a polite smile. He was more cordial than he had been at the hotel the previous night. The two men shook hands. "Back for another year, I see."

"Wouldn't miss it," Brewster said.

"What can I do for you?" Kern asked.

Brewster eyed Murray for a brief second before turning back to the lawman. "We just came from my room in the Belfry."

"And?"

Brewster clasped his hands in front of him as he spoke. There was another fancy watch around his wrist. Even from where he stood, Murray could see it was a silver Bulgari. "It appears," Brewster said, "that I was robbed."

"Robbed?" Kern snapped.

Several citizens nearby repeated Kern's word and moved closer to hear their exchange.

Charlie Brewster nodded. "Someone gained access to my room and stole my Rolex and my emergency fund."

"What do you mean, emergency fund?"

Brewster leaned in toward the chief. "I always keep some extra cash around. Not much, you understand—just a few thousand. In the event, there's ever a problem with a credit card. Can't be too safe, you know."

Kern nodded. "I can't believe something like that could happen. Not at the Belfry."

Brewster shrugged. "I wouldn't make it up."

"No, no, of course not," said the chief. "Let's go take a look at that room."

Brewster and his date headed back to downtown. When Kern moved to follow them, Murray said, "Hey, Chief."

"Huh?"

"What's the deal with him?"

"Charlie Brewster? He's a hot-shot agent from Hollywood. Comes in every year looking for the next big thing. A few years ago, he signed one of these crazies to a four-book deal about fairies or some nonsense."

Murray jerked his head toward the departing man. "You think he might have been the one who bit Abner Dewey and Louise Welford?"

Chief Kern stared at Murray for a moment ,then burst into laughter. "Charlie Brewster is probably the richest man on the island right now. He doesn't need to steal anything."

As the lawman walked away, he continued chuckling and shaking his head.

Murray spun around. He frantically scanned the crowd. He found her dancing alone in front of the fire to Michael Jackson's "Thriller." He sprinted through the crowd toward Louise Welford.

When he reached her, he said, in between gulps of air, "I need to ask you a question."

"Dance with Miss Louise," she said and turned slowly. Her hips swayed to the music, and her hands wriggled in the air. "And you can ask her your heart's desire."

"The bag you kept your money in—"

Louise opened her eyes and said, "Dance! Or no questions."

He looked to the edge of the beach and watched as the chief walked with Charlie Brewster and his date. They seemed to be engaged in conversation.

Murray threw his hands in the air and swung his hips.

"That's better," she said, "much better! Now, what is it you want Miss Louise to tell you?"

"The bag that was stolen," Murray said. "The one that had your money in it."

"Uh-huh." She spun around with her eyes closed.

Murray pulled the small canvas bag from an inside pocket of his jacket. "Did it look like this?"

Louise opened a single eye and paused for a brief second. "No," she said. "It looked like—"

But Murray didn't wait to hear the rest of her answer.

He was already sprinting for downtown.

Chapter 21

Murray dashed up the stairs and burst into the hotel. Charlie Brewster, his date, and Chief Kern were less than a block behind him now.

The clerk, Sebastian, was nowhere to be found. Behind the counter, hanging on the keyboard, was the key for 4E—right where it should. Murray jumped around the desk, snatched the key, and raced for the stairs.

Just as he pulled the stairwell door open, he heard Kern's voice boom through the hotel lobby. "Relax, Charlie. If anyone broke into your room, we'll find them. It's a small island."

By the time the stairwell door closed behind him, he was already on the second floor. He bounded the stairs, two at a time, until he reached the fourth floor. His sides ached, and his stomach cramped from the exertion. It had been some time since he had run this far. Even longer since he'd raced at full speed. He felt like he wanted to vomit.

On the fourth floor, he pushed the door open, immediately turned right, and darted for Charlie Brewster's room. The key slipped into the lock, and he was quickly inside.

With a yank, he opened the top drawer of the dresser and haphazardly tossed the watch inside. His hip banged the drawer closed, and he stepped to the closet.

He took even less care with the small bag of money. He opened a bi-fold door, threw the money to the floor, then slammed the closet closed.

Murray ran from the room, jerking the door closed behind him. The lock clicked as the elevator dinged its arrival to their floor.

He hopped into the stairwell and gently pulled the windowed door toward him. In a moment, Charles Brewster and Chief Kern walked by. Just as he wondered where the redhead was, she came hurrying by.

"They know," a male voice whispered.

Murray jumped at the sound. He turned to see Sebastian on the landing below.

"They know!" Sebastian said. He appeared to be yelling, but his voice was barely above a mumble. He rushed up the stairs and stood next to Murray. "Charles Brewster knows we broke into his room," he whispered.

"He doesn't know it was us."

"But he knows his stuff was taken."

Murray opened his hand to show the key for 4E. "I put it back."

Sebastian's eyes widened. He grabbed the key and shoved it in his pocket. "What do we do now?"

"Now?" Murray pulled open the stairwell door. "We talk with the chief."

"What?"

Murray entered the hallway with Sebastian on his heels.

"Why are we doing this?" the hotel clerk whined. "It's not smart."

"It'll be fine."

"I don't know about this," the hotel clerk mumbled.

They stopped outside Brewster's room and listened for a moment.

"I can't explain it," Charles Brewster said. "It wasn't here before. I swear it."

"He's telling the truth," the woman said. "I saw it."

Chief Kern chuckled. "You saw something that wasn't there?"

"That's right," the woman earnestly said. "It wasn't there, and now it is."

Murray peered around the corner. The three of them—Kern, Brewster, and the woman—stood in front of the dresser. The top drawer hung open, and they were peering into it. Nearby, the bi-fold doors to the closet were pushed fully open.

Sebastian moved around Murray and stood in the open doorway to get a better view of what was occurring.

Chief Kern's head slowly turned toward the visitors, and he frowned. "Look who it is," he grumbled.

Charles Brewster and the redhead faced them.

The chief thumbed toward Murray. "Do you know Mr. Lee?"

"He has shoes on now," Brewster muttered, but his attention had returned to the open drawer. He still seemed confused by the return of his missing watch and money.

"Chief," Murray said, "got a minute?"

Kern's eyebrows lifted. "Chief, is it? You must want something if you're acting polite."

Murray stepped into the room. He had a couple of motives for talking with Kern now.

The first was to get closer to Charles Brewster. He still thought the man suspicious, and Murray wasn't about to give up, even if the watch he'd found was the wrong one and the stash of money wasn't the loot stolen from Louise Welford.

The second motivation was about self-preservation. "I heard Colton mention a boat crossing the river."

"What about it?"

"I think that might have something to do with me."

Kern's lips twisted back and forth as he thought. He crossed his arms before he asked, "How so?"

"The bikers. I think they're the ones trying to cross."

Sebastian watched him with interest now.

The cop abandoned his position near Brewster to stand in front of Murray.

"Chief?" Charles Brewster said. "Can we—"

Kern held up his hand to interrupt the man from finishing.

The tanned man eyed his redheaded companion. The two of them seemed surprised at the cop's sudden dismissal.

Kern's eyes narrowed as he studied Murray. "Okay, buddy. You got my full attention now."

"They're coming for me."

"You?" Kern stepped back and studied Murray with the kind of suspicion that only lawmen can curate—even small-town cops. "Were you one of them or something?"

Murray shook his head. "We had an altercation on the highway coming up from California."

"Altercation?"

"I ran one of them off the road," Murray lied.

"Chief," Charles Brewster whined.

Kern lifted his hand.

Now it was the redhead's turn. She put her hands on her hips. The glitter on her face sparkled as she shook her head. "This is unacceptable—"

The chief's lifted hand turned into a pointing finger, which he extended toward the woman. "Zip it," he said.

The woman's eyes widened, and she immediately quieted.

Kern focused on Murray again. "Those bikers chased you from California up here? To Belfry?"

Murray shrugged. "What can I say? I made an impression."

"You can say that again." The chief rubbed his chin. "That answers one riddle, but why didn't you tell me this sooner?"

"I didn't want to get in trouble." It was another lie, but Murray was on a roll. What was another untruth going to hurt?

"In trouble for what?" Kern asked.

"Running one of them off the road."

Kern smirked. "That's California. I don't care about traffic infractions down there. I only care about what happens on my island."

"Well," Murray said, "I think they're trying to get on the island to get me."

"It must have been some... *altercation* for them to risk their lives crossing the Columbia right now."

"As I said, I made an impression."

"Yeah," Kern muttered. "You did say that."

"What about my room?" Brewster asked.

Kern rolled his eyes. "Anything missing, Charlie?"

The tall, well-dressed man looked about. "No, not anymore, but it was."

"Yeah," the woman added. "It was."

"But it isn't now, so be thankful you got your stuff back." The chief grabbed his shoulder microphone and was about to key it, but he hesitated. He glanced at Brewster and said, "You're welcome, by the way."

Before Brewster could protest, the chief spoke into his shoulder microphone. "Colton," he said.

A moment later, there was a squawk, followed by Colton's voice. *"Yeah, Chief?"*

"Did you find that boat?"

"I did. Abandoned on the shore."

"Find anyone nearby?"

"No, sir. Whoever it was, it looks like they made it safely across and then hightailed it away."

"Keep looking," Kern told his officer. "And be on the watch for any biker types."

"You mean the guys from the other side of the bridge?"

"That's what I mean."

"Roger that."

Kern sucked something through his teeth. "If it is them, you think they came all this way to ask for your proof of insurance card?"

"I think they came for something more substantial than that."

Kern slowly nodded as he considered Murray's words. "Payback."

Charlie Brewster held his watch up to the light. "It's scratched," he whined. "Someone stole my watch and scratched it."

"That's terrible," the woman said and clutched his arm.

Brewster lifted the watch to show the men in the room. "It's a Rolex Sea-Dweller. Do you know how expensive these are?"

Kern rolled his eyes. "Oh, Brewster, you are so cool. I can't stand it." His voice was mocking.

Charles Brewster appeared hurt by the lawman's mocking. "What did I do?"

The chief brushed past Murray on the way out of the room. "I don't have time for this. I've got me some bikers to find."

Chapter 22

It was a fitful night for Murray.

Any creak or groan of the old Belfry Boarding House caused him to bolt awake. As he lay in that semiconscious state, struggling to return to sleep, his ears strained for other noises.

He might hear something such as a dog barking in the distance and imagine a shadowy figure lurking in a nearby yard. As a Satan's Dawg, he'd once been that shadow hoping to avoid inquisitive canines or automatic security lights while on his way to clear the book on some deserving soul.

Was he now that soul deserving of having his entry cleared?

In the eyes of the club, he most definitely was.

Murray hadn't considered that before. Maybe it was from hubris. Or perhaps it was out of willful ignorance. Regardless, he had once been the bookkeeper for the club, but he wasn't the first man to do the job, which meant someone else should have assumed his role by now.

He rolled onto his back and stared up into the darkness.

The club had first sent a crew after him in Pleasant Valley, led by a man with the title of Dawg Catcher. That man was the Satan's Dawgs version of Internal Affairs. Murray had barely escaped him and left him in the hands of the law.

They must have put a new man into his role as well.

Murray wasn't sure which men arrived in Costa Buena, since he didn't stick around to find out. He knew the Bloodhound, Keaton Scoville, was here in Belfry. Scoville wasn't a hitter, though. It wasn't in his make-up. But if the club were short on men, perhaps Scoville would rise to the challenge and take on the role of a bookkeeper.

Throughout the night, these thoughts continued to plague Murray. Several times, he flicked on the nightstand lamp and attempted to read the second Travis McGee adventure, but his worries often pushed back in. He would turn off the light, lay his head on the pillow, and stare up into the darkness.

Sleep came in broken, jagged pieces.

For a brief moment, he listened to the siren of a firetruck. It only sounded for a short burst. Murray didn't remember seeing a fire department on the island, but he hadn't walked its entirety. There had to be many things he hadn't seen yet.

When the morning arrived, and sunlight snuck past the edges of the curtains, Murray reluctantly slipped out of bed.

After waking, he wandered back and forth in his room. This soon turned into fretful pacing. Back and forth. Back and forth.

Even though it was bigger than any prison cell he'd been in, it felt eerily similar. Except he wasn't mandated to stay in this hotel room. Then why was he doing this?

Why am I hesitating to leave?

When he settled on a reason—fear—it didn't sit well with him.

Murray Lee wasn't afraid of any man.

He shuffled into the bathroom and started the shower.

***

Georgia slid a plate of bacon and eggs in front of him. Again, gray-haired patrons filled the Belfry Bruncheonette. The restaurant was alive with the sounds of silverware scraping plates and people happily talking.

Murray bit into a piece of toast when Georgia leaned in front of him. She crossed her arms and rested her elbows on the counter. "You left the bonfire in a hurry last night."

He wondered if she saw him sprinting away.

"It looked like you were competing in the Olympics, the way your arms were pumping back and forth."

That answered his question about being seen.

She pushed back from the counter and mimed a runner's arm swing. "Did you run in high school?"

Only from the law, he thought. He continued to chew his toast.

"Where were you going in such a hurry?"

"I thought I left my room unlocked."

She frowned. "You got something valuable in there?"

"My socks."

Georgia laughed. "Socks, he says." She looked around and made sure no customers needed her attention. When her gaze returned to his, she said, "No, seriously. Where were you going in such a hurry?"

"My room."

Her mouth twisted. "It's that woman from the bookstore. Shirley Herrick's daughter. What's her name?"

"Anna."

"That's her. I saw you two talking."

"That's not it," Murray said.

Georgia waggled her finger. "Tell that story to someone else. I saw the way she watched you. That woman has got her eyes set on you."

Murray's fork hovered over his hash browns as Georgia walked away.

Officer Colton slipped onto the nearby stool and eyed him with contempt.

"Finish up," the cop said.

"Are we going somewhere?"

Colton nodded once.

"What am I suspected of doing now?"

The officer leaned into him. "You tell me."

There were plenty of things Murray had done in his previous life, but the only illegal thing he'd done since being on the island was enter Charles Brewster's room. And he'd returned the goods he'd mistakenly stolen.

No one would know about the illegal entry unless the hotel clerk spoke to someone.

Murray was operating under the assumption that Sebastian was smart enough to remain silent.

He shoveled some potatoes into his mouth and shrugged.

Colton leaned back and watched Murray. "You don't rattle too easy, do ya?"

Georgia approached and asked, "Get you something, Caleb?"

"Not going to be here long enough."

The server glanced at Murray, then back to the cop. "Should I bring him his tab?"

Colton nodded. "That's a good idea."

Murray gently put his fork down. "Okay, Colton. Why don't you cut to the chase and tell me what this is about?"

"We're going to Forge's."

"What for?" Murray asked.

"Because someone did a little damage to your car last night."

"My car? You think I would damage my own car?"

The cop slipped off his stool and hiked up his duty belt. "No, but to get to your car, they burned down Forge's shop. And Chief Kern thinks you know who did it." He patted Murray's shoulder. "Pay your bill and meet me outside."

Chapter 23

The gas station wasn't entirely burned.

The service bays, however, were destroyed. Inside, Murray's once-white Toyota Tercel was now a blackened hull—a worthless husk.

An odor of an extinguished fire lingered. More than that, though, there was the aroma of burned rubber, scorched plastic, charred wood, and singed cloth. Wrapped around it all was the cloying effect of water transformed rapidly to steam as it displaced the fire.

Near the still smoldering portion of the building, Chief Kern moved slowly around with his head bowed. His feet shuffled in baby steps as his eyes swept the ground. He slowly knelt near the roll-up door and examined some shards of glass. After a few moments, he stood and resumed his shuffling.

Officer Colton stood at the edge of the property. He eagerly spoke with several volunteer firefighters as they wrapped up hoses in preparation to leave. Their bright red engine looked well-cared for even if it looked as if it belonged in an old-time movie.

Murray Lee crossed his arms and took it all in.

"I don't know what happened," Waylon Forge muttered. He stood next to Murray, but his eyes were locked onto his shop. His three-legged dog stood nearby. His attention also seemed to be on the burned building.

"There was nothing that should have started a fire like that." Waylon frowned and shoved his hands inside his overalls. His beanie was pulled low on his head, and gray wavy hair pushed out from underneath. "I just don't understand."

"These things happen," Murray said.

But he didn't believe that. He knew what had occurred. He turned and looked around the neighboring properties. Somewhere someone had to be watching.

This was the work of the Satan's Dawgs. They destroyed his car to keep him on the island. Now, he wouldn't be able to escape.

Except...

Murray turned back to the garage.

It didn't make sense. The bridges were out. He couldn't leave now, anyway.

And how did they know his car was in the shop? There would have been no way for them to know his car needed work.

Did they have an inside man? Was there someone living on Belfry Island providing them with intelligence?

No, that was unlikely. The Dawgs were based in Phoenix, Arizona. There was no need for them ever to have a contact on this island. And Belfry didn't have a motorcycle club. At least, he didn't think they did.

Was it more likely it was an accident—that this was an unfortunate situation to befall Murray? As much as he hated to admit it, maybe it was just that.

"Yeah," Waylon said with a reluctant nod. "These things happen."

Chief Kern approached. "You think those bikers chasing you did this?"

"Maybe," Murray said. "But that's assuming they got on the island and figured out my car was in there."

Waylon eyed him with suspicion.

"Yeah," the chief said and turned back to the smoldering building. "How would they know?"

The three men were quiet for a time. Each was lost in their thoughts as they studied the smoldering building.

Finally, Kern asked, "You make anyone else mad? Someone on the island, maybe?"

"Me?" Waylon asked.

The chief rolled his eyes.

"No," Murray said. Then he thought about messing with the sparkly vampires and their umbrellas. "Not really. No."

"Someone clearly doesn't like you," Kern said. "The fire looks like it started inside your car."

"How's that?"

"Looks like something was placed on the front seat. I'll know more when we get an arson investigator here. It'll have to wait until the bridges open."

Waylon's face turned dark, and he faced Murray. "My shop burned because of you?"

"I didn't do anything."

The shop owner waved his hand dismissively. He wandered away with Wrecker limping by his side.

Murray surveyed the neighboring properties. He was looking for anyone that didn't belong-- someone that might be watching him with intense curiosity. Unfortunately, no one matched that description.

He settled on the fact that someone from the Satan's Dawgs was on the island.

Maybe several of them were here. Somehow, they found his car and burned it. They were ensuring he had no means of escape.

As he stood in the middle of the parking lot, his desire to be a better man was replaced by a more immediate need.

Stay alive.

Chapter 24

Murray's head swiveled as he walked. Everyone was a danger to him now. He immediately discounted those festival attendees who dressed in suits and umbrellas.

The problem, though, was every time he passed one of them, they stopped walking to pretend to be a statue or whatever it was they were trying to do. It highlighted who was playing a vampire and who was a regular citizen. A Dawg paying careful attention to those moving about would easily pick out Murray.

He suddenly froze.

Up the street, standing nose to nose with a suited vampire, was Keaton Scoville, the Bloodhound. His leather and denim clashed widely with the tailored outfit of the person frozen next to him.

Murray instinctively knew Scoville must have come across in the boat that Officer Colton reported. He wondered if anyone else had made it across with him.

Scoville said something, but the fake vampire remained still. This seemed to irritate the Bloodhound, so he barked a profanity. When the suited man flinched, Scoville laughed loudly. Several people turned to see what the fuss was about.

A hand wrapped around Murray's arm and spun him around.

His hand quickly curled into a fist, and he reared back, ready to strike.

Abner Dewey lifted his hands to his face to protect himself. "Whoa, boy! Relax."

Murray dropped his fist. "What do you want?" His tone was sharper than intended.

"You're a jumpy one, ain't you?"

He glanced back over his shoulder. Keaton Scoville had vanished.

"Any luck with the search?" Dewey asked.

Murray reluctantly faced him. "For your watch?"

Abner nodded. "I'll admit it. You got me excited about the prospect of getting it back and keeping half the insurance money for myself."

"I haven't found it yet," Murray said and peeked over his shoulder again. "But I'll stay after it."

"You do that, son. You do that."

Abner patted him on the shoulder and crossed the street. Murray turned back to where Scoville had been, and the Bloodhound was returning, but this time there were two other Dawgs with him.

Pups, Murray thought. In other words, prospects. And those men would be eager to make a name for themselves to earn their club patch.

The three Dawgs eyed him like he was a cornered rabbit, and they hadn't eaten in some time.

Murray hurried into the nearest store, The Thirst of the Mind. For a brief second, he expected to bump into Flat Edmund, but he remembered the cardboard vampire was now safely perched behind the counter—where both Shirley and Anna Herrick stood.

"Hi, Murray." Anna's words rang throughout the store.

"Mr. Lee," Shirley said coldly.

He stole a final glance up the street and saw the pack of Dawgs head his way.

He spun and trotted through the store. "I need to go out back."

"What for?" Anna asked as she moved from behind the counter.

"Did your friend find you?" Shirley asked.

Murray paused. "My friend?"

The store owner said, "I ran into him last night after I left the bonfire."

"Did you tell him where to find me?"

"How could I do that?" Shirley asked. "I don't know where you're staying."

"But you told them about my car being in Forge's shop."

"I thought maybe Waylon could tell them where to find you."

"The fire," Anna said. "Do you think your friend is responsible?"

"Whoever it was isn't my friend," Murray said. He hurried to the back of the store.

"Mom!" Anna hissed. "How could you?"

"He seemed like a nice boy," Shirley Herrick muttered. "Terrible dresser, but a nice boy."

Murray shoved the back door open and stepped into the alley.

Anna called, "Wait," but Murray didn't.

He searched in both directions. Finding it clear, he headed toward the Belfry Boarding House.

"Where are you going?" Anna asked as she jogged alongside him.

"I've got to get away from here."

"Why? Who is looking for you?"

Murray shook his head as he loped through the alley. Sprinting wasn't necessary right now. He needed to keep his wits. Three Dawgs were roaming free now. Could there be a fourth? Maybe a fifth?

Running full out would not allow him to be as aware as if he took a little more time. He scanned every movement, and he occasionally glanced behind him.

"Why won't you tell me?" Anna said.

"You should go back."

"Because I'm some sort of fragile flower?" She stopped running.

He had no intention of stopping, but when he glanced back to say something to her, he saw them. The three Dawgs piled out of the rear of the bookstore. One of the prospects, the lanky one named Stank, stood with his arms thrust forward.

Murray yanked Anna by the hand as a gun fired, and a bullet whizzed by.

"They're shooting!" Anna hollered.

At the opposite end of the alley, Keaton Scoville slapped Stank and took his gun from him.

So the Dawgs didn't want to kill him. At least not with a bullet in a Belfry alley.

It was time to throw caution to the wind. Murray's hand tightened around Anna's wrist, and they sprinted towards the alley's opening.

From behind them, the Dawgs hollered, "You're dead, Beau! You hear me? *Dead!*"

Chapter 25

Once they were free from the alley, Murray turned on the side street—he didn't catch the name—and returned to the main strip of shops.

He hesitated while deciding what to do.

There was no friend to ask to hide him. There was also no place on the island he called home.

The Belfry Boarding House was a temporary place to rest his head, and he didn't want to lead the Dawgs in that direction. He still might need to return there.

His car was burned out, so there was no reason to run to Forge's and collect it.

And since there was no chance of getting off the island due to the bridges still being out, it felt like he was about to run in a giant circle.

Which left him a big question of where to run.

Should he turn and fight?

Yes, he decided. Fight now while he had energy and his wits.

He turned to face his pursuers and saw them leaving the alley. They immediately turned toward him and sprinted.

Three against one, he thought. *I've fought against worse odds before and survived. Like that time in—*

"Let's go!" Anna ordered.

She yanked him by his arm, which caused him to stumble off the curb and into the street. Once he regained his balance, he ran with her onto the opposite sidewalk.

Anna was a taller woman and running at full stride. He did his best to keep up with her, but it was clear she was holding back so he could run with her.

Well-dressed vampires and casually attired Belfry citizens watched with mouths agape as the two darted, side-stepped, and rushed by.

"Beau!" a voice rang out from behind them.

Murray refused to look back.

Several more male voices shouted, "Beau," now. It sounded like more than three, but he wouldn't glance back. Doing so would slow him down, and he was already struggling to keep pace with Anna.

There were so many voices hollering "Beau" now that they sounded like a pack of baying beagles.

Edgar Allen, the owner of The Lost Toys, stood under the canopy of his store and watched the chase. He waved as Beau and Anna passed by, but he didn't say anything. There wasn't time for him to do so.

"Here," Anna said and cut around the corner.

No! he thought.

She was leading him towards the police station. He didn't want to go there.

Getting tangled up with the law at any time was the wrong decision. Not only would the cops definitively learn who he was, but they also couldn't keep him separated from the Dawgs forever.

And if that was the case, someone was going to die.

Murray was sure it wouldn't be him, but he didn't want another death on his hands. He'd already had enough in his life.

When he slowed, Anna looked back with surprise. "What are you doing?"

"Not the cops," he said through gulps of air. He waved a hand. "I don't want them involved."

"I'm not stupid," she said, then looked over his shoulder. Her eyes widened, and she yelled, "Hurry!"

It frustrated him that she wasn't even breathing hard.

She thrust out her hand, but he pushed it away.

"Go," he said. "I'm right behind you."

The two of them ran again.

The baying of the Dawgs continued for several twisty blocks. Anna knew the island's neighborhoods better than he or their pursuers. She cut down sidewalks when appropriate, ran through yards when necessary, and once double backed over ground they had already traveled.

Murray wasn't sure how long they had been running from their pursuers, but at some point, Anna ran them into the yard of a little yellow house. They continued into the back and stayed silent as they huddled near a small metal shed.

He bent over in pain. His sides ached, and his stomach hurt. His back arched as he sucked desperately for air.

"Stand up," she said. "You'll breathe easier."

He glared up at her.

"Or don't," she said. "You're the one who has to live with the pain."

Murray straightened and put his hands on his hips. The breathing didn't feel any more comfortable.

"Lift your arms into the air," she said.

"Huh?"

"Do it."

He did as she ordered, and, amazingly, the breathing came more naturally. They stood that way for a couple of moments. Both remained silent and listened for the Dawgs. When they didn't hear or see their pursuers, Murray said, "I think we lost them."

Anna said, "Yeah. I think so."

Murray lowered his arms. "Where are we going?"

She walked toward the back of the little house. "We're already here."

Without hesitating, she opened the back door and walked in.

Murray stole a final glance around the neighborhood, then trotted up to the house.

Chapter 26

"Who's Beau?" Anna Herrick asked as she pulled two cups from the cupboard.

"It's a long story," Murray muttered. He tilted his glass and finished the last bit of water. He'd already had a refill. His breathing had returned to normal, and he was no longer sweating.

They were in the kitchen of Shirley Herrick's home, which was several blocks away from Main Street and The Thirst of the Mind.

In the living room were two recliners that faced a large TV. On the walls hung a variety of posters and framed photos from the *Evenfall* series. Stacks of books, most of which seemed to be vampire-related, were littered about the room.

Before the coffee started, the house smelled like fake flowers, the kind that come from a spray can. It reminded Murray of his grandmother. She often sprayed a floral scent throughout her home. Spring in a can, she called it.

Anna placed an empty coffee cup on the dining table in front of Murray. On the side of the mug was a black cat peering up from its bottom.

She sat across from him with an also empty mug. Hers, too, had a cat, but it was a mangy-looking thing with its paw extended. Near its bottom was a caption that read *Talk to the Paw.*

Anna noticed Murray's gaze. "My mom's," she said and picked up the cup. "If you don't like cats, I can give you a mug with Edmund's face on it."

He shook his head. "This cup is fine. It got me thinking about my cat, is all."

"You have a cat?" Anna said, genuinely surprised.

"I do." He thought about the tabby he left behind in Costa Buena. "At least, I did."

The coffee pot on the counter gurgled as it continued to brew.

"So, Murray with a cat," Anna said, "I think you owe me some sort of explanation about what's going on. I was shot at and chased by a horde of bikers. That doesn't happen to me every day."

"Has it ever happened?"

"You're ignoring my question."

And she had ignored his, he noticed.

He stared into the bottom of his empty mug. Anna didn't seem scared when the shot rang out. She mentioned she had been in trouble with an ex-husband while living in Texas. Now he wondered what kind of problem that was. She hadn't panicked during their escape from the Dawgs. He had underestimated her as the daughter of a bookstore owner.

Anna rested her arms on the table and leaned toward him. He got the sense she was trying to search his down-turned eyes.

"By the way you responded," Anna said, "I think you've been shot at before."

"I can't tell you much," he said.

She clucked her tongue, then flicked the handle of her mug. "You've avoided telling me anything. You still haven't told me who Beau is."

Murray looked up. "If I tell you about me, about my past, it'll put you in harm's way. Do you understand?"

Anna crossed her arms and gnawed on her lower lip. "We all have a past."

"Trouble in Texas. That's what you said."

"That's right."

"Ex-husband you needed to escape?"

She shrugged. "Something like that."

Murray watched her. She wasn't giving up her truth any more straightforwardly than he was. "I had some trouble down south, too," he said. "Some men I needed to escape."

"Are those the ones that shot at us?"

"Some of them."

"There are more?"

He nodded.

Her face flattened. "What did you do?"

Murray couldn't tell his full story to her, but he had to give her enough to explain the kind of danger he was in.

"I crossed them."

"How'd you do that?"

"I crossed them. That's all you need to know. For your safety."

She sighed and returned to gnawing her lip. It was evident she didn't appreciate being given the barest details.

He knew the feeling.

The coffee pot continued to burp and hum as she thought. Murray returned to studying the image of the black cat on his coffee mug.

Anna wiggled the handle of her cup back and forth when she asked, "You were running from them when you came to Belfry?"

He nodded. "Just before the bridge washed out."

"Now, they're here, and they want to what? Kill you?"

"Or worse."

"What's worse than killing?"

"There are a lot of things worse than dying."

She thought about it for a moment, then said, "Yeah. I guess there are."

The coffee pot gurgled a final time, and Murray stood. He poured them both a cup, then settled the glass carafe onto the burner.

Anna wrapped her hands around her cup and carefully asked, "Those men, if they catch you, will they do horrible things to you?"

He sipped his coffee before responding. "If they catch me, it will be purposeful and painful. It won't be quick. They'll enjoy their time with me."

She pushed her cup away. "What are you going to do?"

"They burned my car, so I've got to figure out a new plan."

"Can you call your insurance company?"

He smiled. "I didn't have insurance."

"Even if you did," Anna said, "you've got to get away from those men today. You can't wait around for an adjuster."

"I'm stuck," Murray said. "I need to get across the river. From what I've heard, it's dangerous for a small boat with the water the way it is."

"More dangerous than a group of men with guns?"

"What's my option?" Murray asked.

She sipped her coffee. "If you're not waiting for your car, why not cross now?"

"At night seems best. Who knows if they got someone on the other side?"

"That's not what I mean. Why not cross back into Oregon over the bridge that's under construction?"

Murray stiffened. "A person can walk across it?

She nodded. "Cars can't go over, but the construction workers can. It's not easy, but it can be done."

If that's true, he wondered, why hadn't the Dawgs just walked across the bridge onto the island?

"Want to go see it?" she asked.

"I do, but not now. When it gets darker."

"Are you worried about getting seen?"

"I stand out."

"Yeah, you do." Her eyes narrowed, and her head tilted. "You most definitely do."

"What are you thinking?"

"I've got an idea."

"What?" Murray asked.

"If I tell you," she said, "you'll only argue. Better if I just get started."

"Now, wait a minute."

"You stay here," she said and stood. "While I'm gone, take a shower and shave."

"Shave?"

Anna put her coffee cup in the sink. "There's a razor in the shower you can use."

"Do you use it for your legs?"

"Don't be a baby," Anna said. "It'll work fine on your face. You want to get out of here alive, don't you?"

He did.

"Then do what I say. Shower and shave. That's an order." She pointed at him. "I'll be back as quick as I can."

Reluctantly, he nodded.

She paused at the door. "By the way, what size pants do you wear?"

Chapter 27

Anna Herrick returned in an hour. When she did, she had a large, brown paper bag tucked under an arm.

"I've got it all planned out," she said and placed the sack onto the kitchen table. She put her hand into the bag and asked, "Do you trust me?" She playfully lifted her eyebrows several times.

Murray put his hands on his hips. "No," he said. "Not at all."

He was freshly washed and shaved, but he was back in his funky and slightly damp Rockafellers T-shirt, dirty jeans, and wet Converse tennis shoes.

"You don't have many other options," she said.

Anna withdrew several items from the bag and spread them out on the dining room table—a suit jacket, pants, a white shirt, and a red tie. The final item she lifted from the bag was a pair of black loafers with socks tucked into one shoe.

Murray's lip curled, and he pointed at the clothes. "I'm not wearing that."

"Fine," she said. "It's not my head those guys are after."

He waved his hands in front of him as if he were putting out a fire. "I've never worn a suit in my life."

"Not even when you were in court?"

His eyes slid to hers. "What are you implying?"

She shrugged. "I'm not implying anything."

"Then what's with the crack about court?"

Anna folded the empty brown paper bag. "Be honest, Murray. Those guys who are out there... there are more of them, by the way. The last count I had was eight. They seem to be intent on finding you. Why would they care so much about a guy like you?"

"I ran one of them off the road," he said.

"Unlikely."

"Back in California," he added weakly.

She tossed the folded sack on the counter, then sat at the table. "And these tough motorcycle guys chased you all the way to Belfry?"

"That's right," Murray said.

"It doesn't smell right."

"What do you mean? They want payback, so they followed me."

Anna crossed her arms. "Yeah? How many of those guys do you suppose have outstanding warrants?"

Probably a few, Murray thought.

"And how many already have a couple felony strikes against them?"

Except for the prospects, all the Dawgs had been convicted of at least one violent crime. He knew that to be a fact.

"You think anyone would risk their freedom for revenge against a terrible driver?"

Murray's brow furrowed. "What makes you an expert on what they would do?"

"I know their type."

He watched her for a bit until he made the connection. "Your ex-husband?"

She nodded.

"Where's he at now?"

"He's in Walls Unit."

Walls Unit was the nickname for the Texas State Penitentiary at Huntsville.

"What's he doing there?" Murray asked.

"Life."

Murray rubbed his freshly shaved chin. "Cute. When I asked what happened to your relationship, you said life."

She shrugged. "I didn't lie."

"What's he in for?"

"He killed a man during a robbery."

"So that's why you came up here."

She nodded.

"You're hiding out, too."

"Not me," Anna said. "I'm clean. He did that job on his own, and that's how he's going to do his time. I'm not waiting around in Odessa while he serves life in Huntsville."

It was a cold statement, but at least he knew a little more about her.

"What's your plan?" Murray asked.

"You put these clothes on, and we go to the movies."

His brow furrowed. "The movies festival?"

"Three movies." She held up as many fingers. "Played back-to-back. The marathon starts in an hour. You'll be safe inside a darkened theater. All we've got to do is get you inside there. The streets will be empty. At least, that's what happened when I was here last. If you're moving during that period, you'll be easy pickings for that crew. However, when the movies let out, the streets will be full of vampire wannabes. At that time, you head for the new bridge and cross over. Easy peasy."

"Why not just hang out here until it gets dark?"

"We could, but it's a farther walk to the bridge than if you start from the theater. Besides, why not make up as much ground as you can in the daylight? Then hide in plain sight, if you will."

She was a smart, tough woman with practical insight. What he couldn't figure out was why she was helping him. What did she expect to get out of it?

"You're wondering why I'm helping you."

Murray lifted his hands and showed his palms.

"Because nobody helped my man when he got in trouble. I wasn't around when it went down. Maybe if I were, he wouldn't have gotten pinched. Who knows? Maybe he would. But the way I figure it, if I do right by you and get you back to your girl, then maybe my life will turn out okay. Does that seem stupid?"

He didn't think so. He'd spent the last several weeks trying to live a better life, trying to make some sort of amends for the man he had been. Some of it was to prove to Daphne Winterbourne that he was a decent man, but mostly it was to prove the same thing to himself. So for her to want to do the same thing didn't sound stupid in the least.

Murray lifted the suit jacket. "You really think this will work?"

"What have you got to lose?"

Chapter 28

Anna was right. He *had* worn a suit for court appearances, but he always hated it.

Murray only owned one suit in his life, and he'd left it behind in Arizona with his old life. It was a blue pin-striped get-up that a lady attorney chose while he was in his early twenties. The court date happened after he patched into the club, and the Dawgs paid for it. When he went to court, he had to put his long hair into a ponytail and trim his beard. She said the suit made him look presentable. He thought it made him look tame—like society had neutered him.

After he got into trouble with Agent Ekleberry, he once again stood before a judge in that suit and tie—neutered by the system this time.

However, after agreeing to cooperate with the feds and slipping into the Witness Protection Program, he thought at least one good thing would come from the moment—he'd never be in a suit again.

Yet here he was.

Standing in front of a full-length mirror in Shirley Herrick's bedroom, Murray Lee assessed himself.

The pants he wore were baggy around the waist, and they bunched about his ankles. The jacket pulled under his armpits, but it buttoned as it should around his chest. The white shirt was too tight around his neck, and he had to leave the top button unfastened.

Around his neck was a solid red tie with a skinny knot. He still remembered how to tie it in the fashion the lady lawyer showed him.

On his feet were the pair of black loafers that fit far better than he would have imagined. He wriggled his toes at the end of them. The shoes didn't bind or bite.

At least, the socks and shoes were dry. That was a heck of an improvement over what he was wearing.

Murray gave himself a final, disapproving assessment before saying, "I look like a dork."

Anna stepped around the corner to appraise him. She kept her hands behind her back. "You look like a dork who nobody will recognize."

"Maybe," he said and unbuttoned the suit jacket.

"You don't look like a vampire, though."

"I don't?"

"You look like a banker," she said and exposed her hands. In her right hand was an aerosol can. "Close your eyes."

He did as he was told and soon felt a wetness on the left side of his face.

"The heck?" he grumbled.

"Don't move," she said.

The aerosol hiss continued for several moments, and Murray felt the wetness grow on his temple, cheek, and chin. Finally, it stopped, and Anna said, "Open up."

Murray stared at his reflection. "No," he said flatly. "Definitely not. Now I look stupid."

"That's how vampires are supposed to look."

"They're not supposed to sparkle," he muttered.

"These vampires do."

Purple glitter covered the left side of Murray's face. He lifted his hand to his cheek, but Anna slapped at him.

"Don't touch it! You'll ruin it."

He smirked.

"You look better," Anna said as if already losing herself in thought. "But now you look like a banker vampire." She crossed her arms and tapped her finger against her front teeth. Eventually, she said, "It's the hair."

"What's wrong with my hair?" Murray whined.

There it was again—the whine. He'd been on Belfry only a couple of days, and he was turning into a whiner.

"Your hair looks like you comb it."

He huffed. "That's because I do."

Anna clucked her tongue and walked away. When she returned, she had a can of hair spray and a brush. "Sit on the edge of the bed," she ordered.

He thought about arguing, but he was already in the mix. Warily, he sat.

For several minutes, Anna brushed and sprayed. Then she mussed his hair by wriggling her fingers in it. She stepped back to appraise her work, shook her head in frustration, and stepped forward to repeat the process.

Brush and spray. Brush and spray. After a final muss, she pointed toward the mirror. "Take a look."

Murray stared at his reflection. He couldn't decide if he should laugh or cry. His hair was poofy and purposively disarrayed, and not at all cool. He looked as if he had stuck his finger in a light socket.

"Getting better," Anna said.

"Better?" Murray moaned. He winced at the whine in his voice. He needed to get off this island fast.

"But something is still missing."

When he reached up to touch his hair, she smacked his hand.

"Leave it alone," she said. "It's fine."

"I don't look like me anymore."

"That's what you want," she said. "You want to look different from who you were, but you want to fit in with everyone else."

He stared at the image in the mirror. "I look like a fool."

"No, you don't," she said. "Maybe it's the teeth."

"What's wrong with my teeth?"

"Nothing, but I didn't get you any vampire's teeth."

Murray rolled his eyes. "I'll keep my mouth closed."

Anna stood behind him with her arms crossed and studied his reflection. "Okay, do that. But something is still missing. You don't look fancy enough."

"Thank God," he muttered.

"No," she said. "We need you to look spiffy."

"Ugh."

"Wait here," Anna said and left the room. He heard her rummaging in the room next door.

While she was gone, he lightly patted his poofy hair. It felt crunchy. Then he touched the glitter on the side of his face. There was no wetness to it now. Instead, it felt sharp, as if he had little pieces of gravel stuck to his face. He forced a smile, and his left cheek felt as if it was cracking.

Anna returned and caught him smiling. "What are you doing?"

"Nothing," he said and scowled.

"It seemed as if you were enjoying your new look."

"No, I wasn't."

She chuckled. "Okay, tough guy. Stick out your left hand."

He reluctantly did so. The woman was starting to irritate him.

"I want this back," she said as she strapped a leather band around his wrist and fastened it into place. "The rest of the clothes you can keep, but this is mine."

When she finished, she stepped back to check him out in the mirror. But Murray wasn't interested in his reflection. He was more intrigued by what was attached to his arm.

It was a silver watch with dings around its bezel. The leather band was reddish-brown and nicked with experience. He stared at the brand name at the top of the timepiece.

"It's a Rolex," Murray muttered.

"Uh-huh," Anna said as she smoothed Murray's suit jacket. "It was my husband's."

Murray said, "Abner Dewey might disagree with you."

Her eyes snapped to his, and she stiffened.

The first time Murray saw her, he thought she had the build of a volleyball player. Anna Herrick was a tall woman with broad shoulders and bright eyes. Standing next to her now, with a new reference in mind, he realized she might make an imposing figure in the right situation.

Both Abner Dewey and Louise Welford were elderly and short. When they described their attacker as big, it wouldn't take much to tower over them.

Abner said his attacker sounded as if they were trying to disguise their voice. Anna would have to do that, or she would let her victims know she was a woman.

"Why'd you do it?" Murray asked.

She stepped back from him. "What are you talking about?"

"If I look around this house, will I find the bag of money you stole from Miss Louise?"

She stepped toward the door. "You can't search our house."

"You robbed a couple of old people."

"Look at you," she said with a smirk. "You're hiding from some bikers. For who knows what?

I bet it's a lot worse than stealing from people who've got enough."

Murray lifted his hands. "Relax, Anna. I'm not going to turn you in. Just tell me why."

She leaned against the door frame and crossed her arms. After a time, she blew out a long, slow breath. "My mom," she said.

"Shirley?"

"She doesn't make any money with the bookstore. There's no way to sell that many vampire books to keep the lights on."

"So, you robbed Louise and Abner?"

Anna shrugged. "Abner's one of the wealthiest people on the island. He's always going on about his watch. I figured if I took it, maybe I could get a few bucks for it. I looked them up online and saw how much they're worth."

"But Edgar wouldn't buy it from you."

"How'd you know I took it to him?"

"Lucky guess."

"He said the town was too small to buy something that easily identifiable."

"That's why you stole from Louise?"

She shook her head. "I figured since I was in a vampire get-up, I might as well do two for one. Besides, Louise is wealthy, too. She's not going to miss one day's worth of sales. It'll help out my mom, though."

"Why bite them?"

She shrugged. "I had to make it look like one of the visitors. The only way to do it was by biting. I didn't mean to bite Abner so hard, but the man was so jittery. I was only trying to leave a mark, not break the skin."

Murray caught a glimpse of his reflection in the mirror. The poofy, glittery image was too much for him to take, so he looked away. "Why help me then? And don't give me the bit about karma because I'm not going to buy it."

She shrugged. "I miss it."

"Miss what?"

"The rush. The excitement of being around my husband. There was always something going on. Our life was hard, for sure. It was never easy, and it seemed like we were always on the run. Then he goes away for life, and suddenly everything just seemed so boring. I figured I would come up and stay with mom, but that didn't change anything. Belfry is quiet. Too quiet, if you know what I mean."

Murray understood what she meant. The switch from "the life" to normal was jarring, especially if it was something a person didn't want. But Murray embraced the idea of living free of drama. He didn't want to have to live his life always looking back over his shoulder.

"So helping me..." he asked.

Anna shrugged. "Seemed like fun."

He stared at Abner Dewey's watch and struggled to determine what was right in this situation.

Anna grabbed his wrist. "The movies start in thirty minutes. I need to get changed."

She hurried into the next room and banged the door closed behind him.

Murray was left alone with his thoughts.

Chapter 29

"So… Edmund is in high school?" Murray asked.

"Yes," Anna whispered.

Shirley Herrick leaned around her daughter and angrily shushed Murray.

He returned his focus to the movie screen. They were halfway through *Evenfall,* and he was already having trouble paying attention to the film.

It was heavy with teenage melodrama, and the actors were overly beautiful. The actress who played Adela—the object of Edmund's affections—was supposed to be an ugly duckling who later transforms into a beautiful swan. The action that altered her into a stunning young woman was the simple act of removing her reading glasses.

During that scene, several in attendance moaned in awe. When Murray snickered and rolled his eyes, Shirley threw popcorn at him. It was clear the fans of these movies saw something that he didn't.

"Don't worry," Anna whispered, "I don't get it either."

Before the start of the movie, she stepped out of her bedroom in an attention-seeking dress that highlighted her broad shoulders. "What do you think?" she asked.

Unfazed by her blatant attempt, he asked, "You're not dressing in a suit like the other female vampires?"

Anna smirked. "And cover up this body?"

He ignored her question and pointed to her white tennis shoes. "Those don't go with your dress."

"I'll carry my shoes with me and switch into them at the theater."

"Won't the Dawgs notice you're the only one not in a suit?"

She scooped up a pair of red heels and left the room. He followed her to a closet, where she pulled out a long, black raincoat. She whipped it around and slipped her arms into it. After buttoning it up, she fastened the belt around her waist.

"They'll never even notice the red dress," she said.

Murray eyed the slicker. "Is that what you wore when you attacked Abner and Louise?"

Her eyes narrowed, and her voice hardened. "Get over it, Murray."

And he did.

There wasn't much he could do at that moment about Abner Dewey's stolen watch or Louise Welford's pilfered funds. At the top of his priorities was getting off the island in one piece. If he could do it without the Dawgs knowing about it, so much the better.

Outside the house, Anna popped open a bright pink umbrella and handed it to Murray. "Here."

He pulled back in mock horror. "I'm not holding that."

"You are," she said, "or your hair is going to fall flat, and that glitter is going to run. Then your friends will know you aren't one of the attendees."

His shoulders slumped, and he reluctantly grabbed the handle of the umbrella. It rested against his shoulder.

She slipped an arm under his and said, "Let's go, handsome."

He quickly pulled his arm away. "You know I have a girlfriend." Acting chaste felt both odd and weirdly satisfying at the same time.

"I'm not a rube," she said, "so quit treating me like one. You need to sell that we're a couple, or otherwise, it'll look weird."

"We'll be fine walking side by side."

Anna clucked her tongue before muttering, "Whatever."

Outside on the sidewalk, he felt suddenly vulnerable. He had nothing for protection. Worse, he looked silly. He couldn't imagine it getting any worse.

"Now, we need to walk like them," Anna said.

"Huh?"

"Long strides," she said, walking away from the safety of the umbrella. "And thrust your hips like this."

Her hips bounced from side to side as she strode down the block.

Murray stopped walking and watched her. "No," he emphatically said. "I won't do that. Not a chance."

Anna spun around and hurried back under the umbrella. "If you don't walk like that, you'll stand out. And all this—" She motioned toward his hair and glitter. "—will be for naught. Is being cool more important than being alive?"

He glanced around. He didn't want to look foolish. However, his hair was teased, and glitter covered the left side of his face. Looking absurd was in the rearview mirror. He might as well lean into being a pretend vampire.

Murray shook his head in disgust, muttered, "Fine," then took an exaggerated stride.

Anna giggled with glee as she matched his elongated strides.

They traipsed in that fashion to the movie theater. Several members of the Satan's Dawgs wandered through downtown, but none of them offered more than a passing look of bewilderment.

Near Batty for Crafts, Chief Kern and Officer Colton braced a couple of Dawgs. It was clear they were asking them questions about being on the island, but the gang members were less than cooperative. The chief seemed to be less than thrilled with their responses.

But no one even suspected it was Murray as he and Anna paraded through downtown. Once they arrived at the movie theater, which sat next to the Belfry Boarding House, they simply strolled in and joined the eager crowd.

After Anna had hung her coat and switched her shoes, Shirley Herrick found them. She grabbed her daughter by her hands and held them out. "You look so beautiful. I'm glad you came." When she turned to appraise Murray, she seemed genuinely taken aback. "Mr. Lee?"

He nodded.

"You look positively MacCrain." She held a hand to her chest.

"You look nice, too," Murray said.

Shirley wore a dark gray pantsuit with matching shoes. She dismissively waved her hand at him. "Oh, I didn't have any time to change. I had to get ready at the store." A bell dinged, and her face brightened. "It's about to start. Let's hurry."

Now, there were still roughly thirty minutes left in the first movie.

For a time, he worried about the Dawgs bursting into the theater, finding him, and dragging him out, but he'd marched right through them. They had no idea he was inside the movie theater. He felt safe for now.

All he had to do was hang out in this crowd of vampire wannabes and watch two more silly movies until darkness fell. Then he could slip into the night and walk over the bridge and back onto the mainland.

He would deal with whatever happened then, but at least he wouldn't be stuck on Belfry.

Murray returned his attention to the movie.

After several minutes of wooden acting, he leaned over and asked Anna, "Why does Edmund pout so much?"

Shirley Herrick threw another handful of popcorn at him.

***

After the first movie ended, the theater's lobby filled with mostly suited vampires of both genders. There were a couple of people in jeans and plain white T-shirts—the uniform of a lycan while in polite company.

Voices raised in excited chatter. No one bothered to freeze and appear as statues. Whenever a person in a white T-shirt moved about, another in a suit would turn and maniacally hiss. Everyone involved seemed to enjoy the moment and laughed afterward.

Murray learned that the movie vampires were incredibly stoic and often stood in statuesque poses as the normals—non-vampires—moved about them. They spoke a few lines while their eyes tracked the movement of the normals in the scene. He wondered if that was a purposeful decision based upon the novels, or if it was because the actors appeared to be models who couldn't act. Simply standing still seemed to be the most realistic thing to have them do at any time.

Anna was the only woman in attendance to wear a dress. It signaled she was not a part of this world and, therefore, she stood out. She seemed to relish the attention, even if most of it was negative.

The crowd was enjoying a scheduled thirty-minute intermission while the movies were changed. The theater only had a single screen. Many in the crowd chatted excitedly about the second and third movies—*Crescent Ascent* and *Lunar Mourning*.

The three of them—Shirley, Anna, and Murray—stood by themselves and watched the crowd swirl by.

"So, what did you think?" Shirley asked, almost breathless with excitement.

"It was—" Murray began, but Shirley interrupted him.

"Beautiful, right? Just like I said it would be."

He wasn't going to say that, but he nodded. Agreeing seemed to be easier than arguing with a fanatic.

Nearby the crowd parted, and a woman in jeans and a pristinely white T-shirt approached. Several suited vampires hissed as she approached. She smiled broadly at their contempt.

The pharmacist, Pam Benson, stopped in front of Shirley and crossed her arms. "I knew you'd be here."

"Yeah? Well, you smell like a dog," Shirley said.

"And you look like the dead," Pam replied.

Shirley quickly hissed, and Pam growled. This back and forth continued for several seconds until the two women erupted into laughter.

Murray and Anna glanced at each other and shrugged.

Pam gave an appraising nod to Anna before turning to Murray. Her brow furrowed, and it appeared as if she were trying to recall something. She glanced at Shirley, then back to Murray. "You were the guy who came into my store asking about Spartan."

He nodded.

"The non-believer, right?"

"He's come a long way," Shirley said.

"In two days?" Pam asked as she stepped back to assess him once more.

"I had some help," Murray said.

Pam smirked as she checked out the glitter on his face. "If you were going to be anything, I would have assumed you to be one of us. You seem the kind of man to favor jeans and T-shirts."

"Speaking of jeans and T-shirts," Shirley said, "have you seen all the motorcycle types around town?"

"I have," Pam said. "What do you think that's about? And how did they get on the island? The bridge is still out."

Anna glanced at Murray.

Shirley said, "I don't know, but Chief Kern seems to have his hands full with them. I heard he was going to deputize some of the volunteer firefighters in town to help keep watch on them."

"Can he do that?" Pam asked. "Can a police chief deputize people? I thought only a sheriff could."

"You know Martin. He does what he wants."

A soft *bing-bong* sound played over the speaker, and a tinny voice announced that the second movie was about to begin.

"Don't worry," Anna whispered to Murray. "A couple more movies, and you'll be home free."

"I'm not worried," he said.

But it was a lie. Murray was more than worried.

Chapter 30

He awoke with a start.

The lights in the movie theater were on, and there was an uneasy murmur amongst the crowd.

Murray glanced at Anna. "What's going on?"

"The projector broke."

He looked at Abner Dewey's Rolex. It was barely after three in the afternoon, which meant it was still light outside. "Are they fixing it?"

"They're working on it," Anna said. "They told everyone to remain in their seats."

Shirley leaned forward. "You were snoring," she said with contempt.

"I'm sorry."

"I nudged you," Anna said. "It wasn't that big of a deal."

"How could you fall asleep during *Crescent Ascent?*" Shirley asked. "It's such a compelling movie."

He pointed to the screen. "In my defense, I sort of got creeped out by it."

Shirley gasped, and Anna smiled. Several people in the row in front of them turned to hear Murray.

"I mean," he said. "They're in high school, right?"

"Yes," Shirley said. Someone from the row ahead said, "Duh."

"And Adela is supposed to be how old?" Murray asked.

"Eighteen," Shirley said.

"She's a senior," a woman with shiny, short hair said. "Pay attention, will you?"

Murray held up a hand for her to wait. "And Edmund is attending high school because he was turned into a vampire when he was eighteen. High school is his way of hiding out."

"That's right," several people murmured.

"But in reality," Murray said, "he's a hundred and nine years old."

No one said anything then. They were waiting for Murray to make his point.

"Don't you find that creepy?" he asked. "A hundred-nine-year-old guy is dating an eighteen-year-old."

"No!" several of them said. Immediately, the fans all began chastising Murray at once. Shirley waved them to quiet down.

"You don't understand," Shirley said. "Edmund's eighteen. Adela's eighteen. It's a beautiful love story."

"No," Murray said. "It's not beautiful. Not even close. He's dead, and she's alive. He's a dirty old man preying on a naïve teenager. The whole thing is just gross."

The group in the row ahead of him hissed wildly.

The woman with the shiny hair jumped out of her chair, and her face reddened. "How dare you!" she shouted. "You're an impostor! You don't deserve to dress like a MacCrain. Fake!"

Shirley quickly got up and moved away. Even Anna seemed upset by the sudden singling out of Murray by the *Evenfall* fanatics.

Several people in the row behind him got involved in the discussion now. "What's going on?" one of them asked.

The woman with the shiny hair pointed at Murray. "He called Edmund gross."

A hush fell over the theater now, and everyone looked at Murray.

"That's not what I said," Murray whined. There it was again. What was it with this island? "I said his relationship with Adela is gross."

There was a collective intake of breath from the crowd. One woman cried out, "He didn't!"

"We should go," Anna whispered and reached for Murray.

"Yeah," Murray muttered and started to stand.

But it was too late. Every suited vampire—man and woman—bared their pointy teeth and hissed at him. The effect was oddly silly. At first, he wanted to laugh, but the whole theater was calling attention to him.

Some of the attendees had their phones out and were recording the altercation.

This angered Murray. He'd had enough of these pampered vampire lovers. It was time to jump up and give them a bark. It was time to let them know what a really outraged man looked like. It was time to put the fear of Beauregard Smith into some people.

Before he could move, though, someone poured a large cup of sticky soda over his head. He turned around to catch them, but they were already running away. From behind, he couldn't tell if it was a man or a woman running away.

The crowd erupted in cheers as others began throwing popcorn, *Mike & Ike's*, and *Hot Tamales* toward him. Someone tossed a half-eaten hot dog, wrapper and all, which bounced off his chest. Mustard and ketchup splattered on his white shirt.

Murray jumped from his seat and headed toward the aisle. Anna followed close behind. Shirley ducked for cover as they passed as foodstuff continued to rain down. Mother Herrick yelped in surprise when a mustard-covered pretzel hit her.

Once in the aisle, Anna pushed Murray toward the lobby. The crowd was swelling from below to follow him. They were screaming and hollering with the mass hysteria of a mob.

"Go!" Anna yelled. "Get outside!"

He turned to say something, to plea for calm, but the crowd surged forward. Multicolored sweets and heavily buttered popcorn rained down on him.

"You have to go!" Anna shouted.

Murray turned and burst out of the theater into the lobby. He caught a quick glimpse of himself in the shiny chrome of a post. His poofy hair was matted down now from the soda.

The glitter on his face had washed away. Much of it was now smeared over his left shoulder.

Behind him, the theater doors banged open. "Get him!" someone screamed, and the crowd threw more candy at him.

He raced through the lobby, pushed open the front doors and bolted outside. Down the street were a group of Satan's Dawgs, at least six of them, but Murray couldn't be exact. This wasn't a time for counting.

The doors to the theater opened again, and a swelling mass of fake vampires raced after him, pelting him with assorted sweets.

"Fake!" some of them yelled.

"Impostor!" others screamed.

Down the street, the Dawgs hunched their shoulders, leaned forward, and ran toward Murray Lee.

He sprinted into a neighborhood with the soles of his dress shoes slapping loudly. The mob chasing him cheered wildly.

They were finally going to hunt like the heroes of *Evenfall.*

Chapter 31

The sun was setting, but it wouldn't get dark quick enough for him. Right now, daylight was his enemy. The night would be his friend.

I sound like a vampire, Murray ruefully thought.

He was hiding behind a garage. A coven of suited vampire wannabes hurried through the nearby alley.

They were high on the chase, and their voices boomed with excitement.

"He went this way," a woman enthusiastically said.

"He'll be sorry he ever set foot on Belfry," a man yelled.

"Does anyone know if they fixed the projector?" another woman hollered.

The voices drifted into the distance.

Murray waited until there was silence. Then he leaned against the back of the garage, as the drizzle continued. He needed to find cover soon, or he would be soaked.

If he made a break for the new bridge, the one still under renovation, he might be able to walk across it, as Anna had suggested. However, it was light out. If anyone saw him there, he would be a sitting duck, especially if there were any Dawgs on the other side.

The best thing for him to do was wait until dark. That way, if there were any problems with a bridge crossing, he could adjust his plan and find another way.

He wasn't concerned about the mob of *Evenfall* fans. They couldn't hurt him. Not really. But they would call attention to him and lead the Dawgs his way.

And he didn't want to hurt one of the pretend vampires. Their pursuit might be frivolous, but that didn't mean they should get punched in the face for it.

The best thing he could do right now was to find shelter and get out of the rain.

Returning to the hotel was not an option. The Dawgs might have figured out that's where he was staying. If not, they would likely station someone nearby since there were only a couple of hotels on the island. That's what Murray would have done if he was tracking someone through Belfry.

He wondered if he might be able to convince one of the store owners he'd met to let him hang out until it was dark. It would be a long shot to expect someone to help him after only a quick meeting, but if he'd learned one thing in his short time as a citizen, it was that people tend to be helpful to those they like.

He ran through the list of people he'd met.

Shirley, Anna, and Pam had been at the theater for the movie marathon. Would they still be there if the movie projector wasn't fixed yet? Regardless, Anna had already done a lot for him, and he didn't want to get her more involved. However, he *would* go to the Herrick house and hide there if he could remember how to get back to it.

What about Edgar Allen of The Lost Toys? Would he let him hide out? Unlikely. Unless he could convince the man that the Dawgs were tied into a vampire sect.

What about Georgia over at the Belfry Bruncheonette? Then he quickly ruled her out. She'd made her intentions known, and he didn't want anything to do with that. The old Murray—the guy he was with the Satan's Dawgs—would have jumped at the opportunity to meet a woman like her. But that's not who he wanted to be now, so there was no need to put himself into a situation like that.

For a moment, he thought about Waylon Forge, but the man's shop had burned because of Murray. It was unlikely he would help him in a pinch.

The list of people he knew in Belfry was short. If only he could call Marshal Onderdonk or FBI Agent Ekleberry for help. The thought made him shake his head—former Bookkeeper Beauregard Smith hoping for help from the law.

The law!

Murray straightened with a jolt of hope. Maybe he should run to Chief Kern and hide out in the police station. He hadn't wanted to do that earlier when he was with Anna, but now he had little choice left. Perhaps going to the local cops would be the right choice.

His shoulders slumped when reality collided with his optimism. The police station was small and wide open on the inside. If he hid in there with Kern and Colton, he would be like a fish in a barrel. The Satan's Dawgs could surround the building and plink at those inside until they killed Murray. Kern and Colton would be collateral damage.

As much as he hated the law, he didn't need the deaths of two cops on his conscience. The struggle to be a better man was a drag.

Murray looked up into the gray sky. He wondered how much longer he would need to wait for the night to arrive. He checked his watch.

The Rolex, he thought. He had another option.

Excited by this realization, he pushed off the garage wall and stepped into the alley without ensuring it was clear.

"Hold it right there, rat."

Murray stopped and slowly turned around. He held his hands away from his sides to show he had nothing in them.

The lanky prospect named Stank pointed a semi-automatic at his head. Next to him was a chubby guy that someone in the club had stuck with the nickname of a summer melon.

"He's here!" Honeydew yelled to no one in particular. He struggled to yank a revolver loose from the waistband of his jeans. After several tugs, it came free. With shaking hands, the prospect thrust the gun out. "He's here!" he yelled again.

"Shuddup, Honey," Stank grumbled. Then he waved his gun in small motions toward the sky and said to Murray, "Get 'em up."

Murray slowly raised his hands.

Stank next motioned his gun toward himself and said, "Step to it."

"Yeah," Honeydew said with a jerk of his head. "Move."

Murray stepped forward as he heard a commotion behind him. He glanced back.

A crowd of suited vampires entered the mouth of the alley. Several of them still held buckets of popcorn and large cups of sodas.

"There he is!" someone screamed. "Get him!"

With cheers and hoots, the coven scampered towards the three men.

"Hurry up," Stank growled.

In a panic, Honeydew faced the approaching mob and shouted, "Get back!"

Murray took another step and was now directly between the two prospects. It was something an experienced Dawg would never have let happen, especially the Bloodhound Keaton Scoville. But these were pups who had suddenly found themselves in an overwhelming situation.

What happened next played out in a blur of motion.

To slow the approaching horde, Honeydew lifted his gun into the air with both hands and fired a warning shot to stop.

Even before he pulled the trigger, Stank scowled and uttered the words, "Don't do that, Honey—"

Before the lanky man could finish his command, Murray punched him in the eye.

Startled by the gunshot, the approaching crowd of snack-infused vampires screamed with fear.

Stank, being more professional than Murray had initially given him credit for, did not squeeze the trigger of his gun after being slugged in the eye.

Honeydew, on the other hand, was not as skilled or disciplined as his partner. He swung his gun wildly toward Murray, but the big man had slipped behind Stank, who was now bringing his free hand up to cover his newly injured eye.

When Honeydew's gun fired, Stank squealed and immediately slumped. His hands, even the one with the weapon, clutched his stomach.

The crowd shrieked a second time as it bolted from the alley.

Murray caught the falling prospect from behind and wrenched the gun away from Stank's nearly limp hand. He quickly pointed the weapon at Honeydew, but the other man was no longer a threat.

The chubby prospect stared at the revolver in his hands. He held it on an open palm and stared at it as if he'd never seen it before. It was clear this was the first time Honeydew had ever shot a man.

"Put it down," Murray ordered.

Honeydew never looked up but did as ordered.

"Step back."

The chubby prospect shuffled backward with tears in his eyes.

Murray dropped Stank as if he were a bag of rotten potatoes. The lanky man moaned when he hit the ground.

"Put pressure on his wound," Murray said.

Honeydew rushed toward his fallen friend. When he reached for Stank's stomach, the lanky man smacked his hand away.

"You shot me," he croaked.

"He made me," Honeydew said.

Stank glared at him with his uninjured eye. His other was squinted shut. "He made you shoot me?"

"That's right," the chubby prospect said with emphatic nods. "He didn't stand still."

Murray picked up Honeydew's dropped revolver, then hurried through a nearby yard, leaving the two Dawgs in the alley. He now had two guns and a plan—get to Abner Dewey's house.

It wasn't much, but he felt more dangerous than he had in a long time.

Chapter 32

For several blocks, it was a game of cat and mouse. Unfortunately for Murray, he found himself in the unenviable position of being the rodent.

While running and hiding, he noticed the irony that a bunch of Dawgs, both current and former, were playing this game.

His pursuers must have heard Honeydew's gunshots and sprinted toward their sound. When one of them saw Murray fleeing the alley, they diverted course and gave chase.

While the Dawgs bayed various profanity-laced versions of "You're dead, Beau!" Murray ran through manicured lawns, hopped over cedar fences, and skulked along the various little homes dotting the island.

Occasionally, he glanced back at his pursuers. They gave pursuit, but no one was firing at him now. This made their intentions clear. They wanted to catch him, to bring him back to the club, and make him pay the long way for turning rat.

Not shooting him would be their mistake. The Dawgs had never been into any sort of extended retribution before. When his former self had been their bookkeeper, the accounts were swiftly cleared. Nobody was ever brought back.

Now, in all fairness, no one had ever turned against the club before, so this was unchartered territory. Had the other Dawgs acted as he'd been taught—as he'd carried out his business—then this whole debacle would have ended in the alley with Stank and Honeydew.

Actually, it would have ended in Maine. They had their chance back there. He knew this lust for a particular method of retribution wouldn't continue forever. Sooner or later, someone would realize their mistake, and the crew would start gunning for him. The idea of payback through torture was overrated. Just kill a man and be done with it was how the Dawgs had always operated before. He hoped they wouldn't get back to that mandate too soon.

The rain fell harder now, and his suit jacket felt like a wet towel draped around his shoulders. It slopped around his chest and stomach as he ran. The white button-up shirt was also soaked.

When he cut through one yard, his slick-soled dress shoes failed to grab any traction on the wet grass. He reeled and stumbled before crashing awkwardly to the ground in a heap. Even though his hands were cold and wet, Murray never dropped the guns.

He quickly scrambled to his feet, checked for pursuers, and sprinted away.

"Beau!" the Dawgs howled. "You're dead! You're dead!"

Murray pointed a gun behind him but didn't fire. Hitting and possibly killing one of the Dawgs wasn't his concern. Even a good man had the right to defend himself. These men aimed to do him harm and, therefore, deserved to be shot.

He was running full out, however, and couldn't stop to take the time to aim. If he shot carelessly and hit a citizen, well, he didn't want that on him. The old version of himself—the man the Dawgs were pursuing—would have pulled the trigger without hesitation.

But Murray couldn't do that now. If he was going to pull the trigger, and that was still a definite possibility, he had to be sure to hit what he was aiming at. He leaned forward and ran. His lungs burned, and his stomach ached as he willed his arms and legs to pump harder.

Sirens wailed in the air as Murray sprinted across a street and into the yard of a small, brown home. The first was the unmistakable whine of a police car. Correct that—police cars. It was no doubt both Chief Kern and Officer Colton racing toward the downed Stank.

He shimmied along the side of a house to avoid several cans containing trash, recycling, and yard waste before turning to race toward the alley.

Another siren wailed in the air. Murray guessed it must be from the volunteer fire department. He had been around the island and knew there wasn't a hospital. He wondered if there was a medical clinic where Stank would get additional help. Otherwise, how were they going to get the man off the island? Would they stretcher him across the new bridge? The bridge he had planned to cross earlier?

Yet another reason to wait until darkness fell before trying to escape this little island.

He moved through the alley, entered another yard, and ran toward the next street. Murray avoided straight lines, often zig-zagging with the occasional double-back, as he headed toward Abner Dewey's home.

Unfortunately, he'd turned himself around and was near the commercial area again. Main Street was nearby, and he was in the back of the small grocery store. He could see the burned-out Forge's Repair Shop across the street.

To catch his breath and reset his bearings, Murray paused behind a metal dumpster. The smell of rotting food wrinkled his nose. The rat-a-tat-tat of the falling rain against the big, green box disguised all other noises. This was not a good place to rest. The others might not be able to hear his heavy breathing, but he wouldn't be aware of them if they were creeping up.

Slowly, he stuck his head out around the edge of the dumpster.

There was a loud ping against the metal box near his head. He immediately crouched and withdrew from sight. Instinctively, he knew someone had fired at him even though he hadn't heard the gunshot.

Someone wasn't worried about bringing him in now. The rules of the game had quickly changed.

The falling rain was creating too much noise on the metal dumpster. He needed to get away from it. Hiding here was like being inside a drum line with bad rhythm—he couldn't hear anything that mattered. He'd virtually given up one of his senses in exchange for the illusion of safety.

Two senses were muted if he considered the stink emanating from inside the dumpster.

The last time he poked his head out, he was shot at. He only had two options to move—left or right. Moving left took him toward Main Street. Going right took him back toward the safety of the neighborhood.

If he waited any longer, the shooter—or shooters—would arrive at his location and gun him down as he hid behind a dumpster. It would be a humiliating way to die. Twice as humiliating, dressed like this.

He couldn't wait any longer. Murray took a deep breath, steeled himself for a firefight, and stepped toward Main Street, away from the safety of the neighborhood, which is where the shooters would have expected him to run.

As he ran, he aimed in the direction he expected gunfire. However, nothing came.

Why was that? he briefly wondered.

But he didn't worry about it too long. Instead, he rushed toward the edge of the grocery store, his heart pounding in his ears. When he turned the corner, he found Keaton Scoville, the Bloodhound, waiting. In Scoville's left hand was a simple but deadly weapon—a Smith & Wesson .38 revolver.

Scoville's eyes widened, then quickly narrowed. His lip curled slightly before breaking into a cruel smile.

Both men silently watched the other with guns gripped tightly in their hands.

Scoville was a hard, lean man with none of the physical attributes of his nickname. Thick eyebrows hooded his bright, piercing eyes. A silver ring pierced his left nostril. A shadow of a beard, the kind that male models carefully cultivate, covered his face.

They were under a canopy that covered the sidewalk. A car drove by on Main Street, its tires splashing water almost to the grocery store's path.

"Beau," Scoville said.

"Keaton."

Scoville's right hand was empty and waved as he spoke. "We have a dilemma."

Murray shook his head and lifted his guns. "Two versus one," he said. "No dilemma."

Both men pulled their weapons close to their sides as if to limit the exposure to possible passersby. No one was on the street, though. Most citizens were smart enough to be out of the rain, or they were at the film festival. Some of the angered vampires might be running about, but they weren't his concern now.

Scoville said, "You know as well as I do, one bullet can do the same job as twenty. Dead is dead."

"But you're a terrible shot, Keaton. That's why they made you a tracker and not a bookkeeper. You hit the broadside of a dumpster, but not me.”

The lean man shrugged. “I can hit you from here. Want me to try?”

That was no doubt true, Murray knew. And at this range, if the shooting started, both men were dead.

He needed to do something quickly. Not only were they standing in public, but Scoville could be setting him up. Right now, another Dawg might be sneaking up behind.

Murray asked, “What do you propose?”

“We’re not going to stop,” Scoville said. “You know that.”

“Stop stalling and get on with your proposal.”

“How about you go your way, and I go mine?”

“And then what?” Murray asked. “We meet at another time?”

“Hopefully, not me and you.”

Murray nodded. Scoville wasn’t built for hurting or killing. He was made for tracking. Killing was something the others did.

A quick succession of thoughts ran through Murray’s mind.

I need to hurt him.

Or at least, he should disable Scoville in some way so he could not track Murray again.

If Murray really wanted to be sure, he should kill Scoville.

These were thoughts the old version of himself would have embraced and acted on without hesitation.

Murray knew his internal arguments made sense. Keaton Scoville would continue to hunt him until Murray was either caught by the crew or dead. Neither option was appealing.

But Murray didn't want more blood on his hands.

He'd left a couple of bodies while restarting his life in Pleasant Valley, Maine. That was regrettable, and he didn't want to do it again.

Murray avoided killing anyone in Costa Buena, California. But that was only a few days. How much bragging could he do about that? While with the club, he'd gone almost a year once without killing anyone. Of course, that dry spell was broken by several deaths in a single day. Again, how much bragging could he do?

"I know what you're thinking," Scoville said.

Murray's eyebrows lifted. "Yeah?"

"If I were you, I'd be weighing the odds. *If* you can make it out of here alive. *If* the rest of the crew is on their way. *If* you can shoot me before I shoot you."

"You're not a killer, Keaton."

Scoville shrugged. "Still. You better make a decision soon."

Murray thought about telling Scoville his real thoughts—about wanting to live a better life—but revealing anything about oneself was a weakness in the world of the Dawgs. They would use it against him. It was better to remain silent.

"You don't trust me. I understand that. I'll give you a reason you can."

"What's that?" Murray said.

"Daphne Winterbourne."

Hearing her name uttered by the Bloodhound caused a chill to run up Murray's spine.

"I located your hotel room," Scoville said. "The clerk took some convincing, but he eventually let me into your room. Guess what I found?"

Murray didn't have to guess. He already knew.

Scoville slowly reached inside his leather vest and pulled out several postcards.

Murray fought back the rage he felt, not only at Scoville but at himself for leaving the postcards in the open. What was he thinking? If he wasn't going to send them immediately, he should have torn them up and thrown them away. Murray swallowed and said, "What's the plan? You give me the cards, and we both walk away?"

"Why not?" Scoville said. "I don't want to kill you, and you clearly didn't want to be in the club anymore. Why else would you turn rat?"

"If you didn't want to kill me, Keaton, then why did you shoot at me?"

An embarrassed smile crossed the Bloodhound's face. "It was a stupid decision in the face of opportunity."

"Doesn't the council want me back?"

"Of course they do," Scoville said, "but I knew you wouldn't come back without a fight."

"You're right about that."

"We were friends once," the bloodhound said. "I know how you think."

"We were never friends," Murray said with a shake of his head.

"That's right. We were more than that. We were brothers once. That means something."

Murray knew the truth then. Keaton Scoville had the same religious look that Shirley Herrick had when she spoke about vampires. He was a fanatic for the club. Whatever this momentary promise was, Scoville would never forget. He'd never let him walk away unless he already had a plan.

And he had a pretty good idea of what that plan was.

"What do you say, Beau? I give you these—" Scoville waved the postcards. "And you go. We pretend we never saw each other."

The back of Murray's neck was on fire. "Fine."

"Count of three," Scoville said. "We lower our guns, and I'll give you those postcards. Nice and easy. Nothing to worry about."

"Nothing to worry about," Murray said.

"You want to count it off or me?"

"You," Murray said.

Keaton Scoville grinned. When he opened his mouth to speak, Murray Lee shot him.

Chapter 33

Murray sprinted in as straight a line as possible through several yards. His slick-soled shoes threatened to slip out from underneath him anytime he was on grass. Eventually, he found Shoreline Road and headed toward Abner Dewey's estate. He noticed a small path along the pavement that ran in and out of the trees. This would provide him with more concealment than running out in the open. The sun was low in the sky now.

He checked the watch. It wouldn't be too long for the night to arrive. Then he could make his move.

Murray wasn't concerned with the Dawgs finding him out here on Shoreline Road. He figured they would concentrate more in the city and on the old bridge. Maybe they knew about the ability to walk across the new bridge. He'd deal with that when the time came.

Getting to Abner's would be a place to rest until he could get off this godforsaken island.

Now he had a new concern, though. Did the Dawgs know about Daphne Winterbourne? Had Keaton Scoville told any of the others about the postcards he found? She might already be in danger from the first man they sent after Murray. They sent a man nicknamed the Dogcatcher to Pleasant Valley. He kidnapped Daphne as a way to capture the man Murray was hiding as then. The

Dogcatcher paid dearly for that decision, but he was still alive. Letting that man live was something Murray was seriously questioning at this moment.

He hadn't done that for Keaton Scoville. Perhaps he should have only wounded the man, but the Bloodhound learned how much Murray cared for the woman. That meant she would immediately be grabbed if Murray managed to escape the Dawgs today. He figured Scoville had already committed Daphne's address to memory. And if he forgot where she lived, how hard would it be for a man known as the Bloodhound to find her in Pleasant Valley, Maine?

There were certain things Murray couldn't abide by, and threatening Daphne Winterbourne was at the top of the list.

Killing another man wasn't something he wanted to do anymore, especially when others might already know about Daphne. But just because he didn't want to do it, didn't mean he wouldn't do it.

As soon as he could, Murray needed to alert the U.S. Marshals and the FBI about Daphne being in danger. He could do that from Abner's. That would be his priority.

He trotted along the dirt path and occasionally checked over his shoulder to see if anyone was following. No one was. There wasn't even a car on the road. There hadn't been the previous time he was out here.

When he arrived at Abner's place, he jogged up to the front of the house and knocked. The two guns he'd taken earlier were tucked into his waistband and hidden by his suit jacket.

It took a few moments for the door to open. When it did, recognition wasn't immediate for Abner Dewey. He frowned and said, "I ain't into the movies."

"No," Murray said. "I'm here for—"

"Go up the way. They filmed some of it there, but not here."

"You got it wrong—" When the door began to swing closed, Murray lifted his left hand to stop it. "Abner," he said.

The older man's eyes snapped to the hand splayed open on the front door. Then they drifted to the watch wrapped around Murray's wrist.

"My watch," he muttered.

"I came to give it back."

"Where'd you find it?" he asked.

Murray removed his hand from the door and unfastened the watch. He laid it in Abner's opened hands. "I got it from the person who took it from you."

"You tell Chief Kern about it?"

He shook his head. "No need."

Abner nodded, then said, "Well, come inside. You look like a drowned rat."

Murray stepped inside the house. It was warmer than he would have expected.

"Can I get you something? A cup of tea, perhaps?"

"May I use your telephone?" he asked with extra politeness.

"Sure," Abner said, with a pat on Murray's shoulder. "This way." The older man clutched the watch in his fist and led them through the house.

It was a large rancher decorated with things an older man might find interesting. On the walls of the hallway were photographs of war machines—tanks, planes, and boats—and what appeared to be famous military men. Murray didn't recognize any of them.

The living room was sunken by a few feet and centered around a grand fireplace. A stuffed deer was mounted on a base to resemble rocky ground. In the opposite corner was a white lynx. Its base was constructed to look like snow.

"Phone's on the stand," Abner said and pointed to a black corded telephone. It was made to look like a rotary but had push buttons. It was the only nod to the modern era the phone made.

Murray quickly dialed a phone number. It was answered after the first ring. "Ace Adventures," a woman pleasantly said. "Where your journey begins."

"This is Murray Lee."

There was clicking on a keyboard before the woman replied, "Yes, Mr. Lee."

To not let Abner hear what he was saying, he covered the phone's receiver with his free hand and whispered, "Is there an update on Mr. Onderdonk?"

"He's still indisposed."

"Is he getting better?"

"I'm sorry, sir. I'm not allowed to relay that information—"

"What about Ekleberry?" Murray interrupted.

"Do you mean—"

"FBI Agent Ekleberry," he snapped as loudly as he dared.

"I know," the operator bit back. "It's in your file."

"Oh."

"And we're not supposed to be using titles on this phone. Don't you remember your training?"

"I do," Murray said. "This has been a crazy time."

"Well," the operator said, "before you so rudely interrupted me, I was asking if you meant was Mr. Ekleberry on the way?"

"That's what I meant."

"No, sir, he's not on his way. He is with another customer. He will connect with you as soon as he's available."

Disappointment flooded through Murray. No Onderdonk and no Ekleberry.

"But we're sending a new customer service rep to meet with you."

"Do you mean witness inspector?"

"Sir!" the operator said. "This is an unsecured line."

"Yeah, yeah," Murray said. "What side?"

"Side?"

"Of the island. The bridges are out. I guess you can walk in over the newer one, or you can boat in. How are they getting here?"

"I have no idea."

"Then contact them. You have a way of doing that, right?"

"Yes, we have a way—"

"Tell them when night falls, I'll cross the bridge that's under construction. If they can get there, I'll be in the area. If they're not there when I cross, I'll find a place to hide and call in again."

"Understood."

"Oh, and another thing."

"What?" The woman was irritated with Murray now.

He spent the next several minutes telling her about Daphne Winterbourne and Keaton Scoville's threats against her. When he finished, the woman was no longer irritated. Quite the opposite, she seemed genuinely concerned.

Murray hung up the phone and turned to Abner Dewey.

The older man watched him with curiosity. "You aren't a salvage consultant."

Murray turned his palms up.

Abner pointed at him. "I've seen your types before. Tough guys who find themselves in all sorts of trouble."

He kept his mouth closed. There was nothing to argue about, as it was an accurate statement.

"You're a federal agent, aren't you?"

Murray raised his eyebrows.

"Who are you chasing?"

"I'm being chased."

"The bad guys are chasing the good guys?"

Murray liked the way that sounded, so he let it ride.

"What can I do to help?" Abner asked.

"Let me stay here until night falls. Then I need to get to the new bridge and off this island."

"Heck, son, why don't I make us some coffee? When darkness comes, I'll drive you to the bridge."

"Why would you do that?"

Abner Dewey frowned. "I've got to."

"Got to?"

The older man rubbed a hand over his mouth. "Have you ever been scared?"

Murray shrugged.

"I wouldn't figure a man like you would get scared too often," Abner said. "When I was younger, I didn't intimidate much either. A man wanted to fight, I fought. I never backed down. That was my way. A funny thing happens with age. It steals your resolve, little by little. Before you know it, you find yourself enjoying the comfort that life has afforded you. I didn't realize it until that robber stole my watch. It did a number on me. I think it happened when she bit me."

"*She?*" Murray said.

"Yeah," Abner nodded sheepishly. "It was a woman who did it. I figured you would have discovered that when you got this back." He held up the watch. "That's why I didn't tell no one what she looked like. Why would I? It was embarrassing enough to admit I got robbed.

Then to admit I was scared by a woman pretending to be some fancy-pants vampire. Good lord, I would never live it down. I could barely look at myself in the mirror."

The older man's eyes turned glassy, and he brushed back a tear that never fell. "You know how many times I've been scared in my life? Not a whole bunch, I'll tell you that much. It's not a feeling I especially like. I want to get some of my—" He thumped a fist several times against his chest. "—heart back. Do you understand? I don't want to walk around the rest of my life like I'm scared of my own shadow."

When he stopped talking, Abner Dewey lowered his head as if he was ashamed about what he'd just admitted.

"So," Murray said. "We go after dark."

Chapter 34

The truck bounced along Shoreline Road as country music blared from the stereo. It was a tinny sound that mostly came from a speaker in Murray's door. The speaker mounted in the driver's door near Abner's leg was blown as it rattled and warbled every time a drum was struck during the song.

The resulting music—monotone country music with a busted rattle of accompaniment—felt like torture to Murray. He enjoyed heavy metal and hard rock.

But Abner didn't seem to mind at all. In fact, he seemed to be in high spirits.

"Eastbound and Down," he belted out in a full-throated roar. Then he mumbled the rest of the chorus. This continued throughout the rest of the song. Abner sang out of key with the twangy singer, stumbling over the parts he didn't know, confidently shouting "Eastbound and Down" when the chorus returned before stumbling through the rest of it.

If tonight was his night to die, Murray didn't want this to be the last music he ever heard—a lousy version of country karaoke. He reached for the stereo to turn it off.

Abner angrily slapped his hand. "Never touch a man's stereo, son."

Murray's lip curled, but the older man wouldn't have noticed it in the dark cab.

A new song started, and Abner belted out the first line as if he were at the front of a stage, "Mamas, Don't Let Your Babies Grow Up to Be Cowboys." Then, as before, he mumbled and hummed his way through the rest of the lyrics until he was able to sing the main chorus again confidently.

When they turned southbound to pass through the city, Abner said, "Ain't nobody going to see you at this time of night."

"Drive through Main Street."

"But that's the opposite way," Abner said. "Figured you'd want to get to the bridge and make it across. You being a secret agent and all."

"Head down to the grocer."

"You want to pick up some snacks?" the older man asked. "I get that. I'm a man that likes to have something to nosh on when I travel."

Abner slowed, spun the wheel, and the truck headed westward. It didn't take long for them to see the grocery store. Parked along the curb were two police cars and a fire truck.

"What's going on over there?" Abner asked as he turned the music off. "Looks like someone died."

Underneath the canopy lay a body covered by a tarp. Chief Kern and Officer Colton stood nearby. A couple of firefighters stood farther back. A small crowd of onlookers huddled nearby. Among those onlookers were several members of the Satan's Dawgs.

Traffic backed up along Main Street, and a couple of citizens had taken it upon themselves to wave approaching cars away.

As Abner pulled forward, he rolled down his window and asked the man directing traffic. "What happened?"

The man leaned into the window of the truck. "Darndest thing you've ever seen. A man got hisself murdered."

"Murdered? On Belfry?"

"That's right."

"Any idea who he is?"

"A stranger," the man said. "Nobody's seen him before."

"Huh," Abner said and leaned forward over the steering wheel. As if that simple motion would somehow allow him to see the body hiding under the tarp.

"Chief Kern asked us to detour everyone away from here," the man proudly said. He was obviously pleased with being assigned a task to assist with a homicide investigation. "You know how to get around?"

Abner nodded, turned the steering wheel, and slowly accelerated away.

They were silent for a couple of blocks. Both men were lost in their thoughts. Then Abner Dewey asked, "You know anything about that dead man?"

"What's there to know?"

Abner shrugged. "Dead guy's a stranger. You're a stranger who needs to get off the island in a hurry. I'm not the smartest tool in the shed, but even I can figure out this doesn't smell right."

For a moment, Murray considered the two guns in the pockets of his suit jacket. They were the wrong tools for this moment.

Instead, he figured a little honesty wouldn't hurt any more than what had happened over the past couple of days.

"The dead man is the leader of a crew hunting me," Murray said.

Abner glanced at him, but the truck didn't slow. "What for?" the old man asked. His words were cautious.

"I crossed them when I left."

"You're not a secret agent?"

He figured there was no harm in telling the older man now. "I'm an FBI informant."

"And they wanted some payback?"

Murray nodded.

Abner frowned. "You killed a man because he wanted to kill you?"

"He didn't want to kill me tonight," Murray said. He reached into the inner pocket of his jacket and pulled out the postcards he'd taken back from Keaton Scoville. He held them so Abner could see them.

"What about them?"

"The dead man took them from my hotel room." Murray's thumb was underneath Daphne's name.

Abner squinted at the address. "That your woman?"

Murray nodded.

The older man glanced at Murray sideways. "It was sort of dumb writing to her in the first place. Leaving the postcards in your room was just asking for trouble."

Murray didn't say anything after that. He only thought about Marshal Onderdonk's rules.

Do not contact people from your old life.
Do not visit places from your old life.
Do not develop habits from your old life.

He'd been selfish in wanting to contact Daphne. He should never have written her. It was too risky. He'd written to her a couple of times already while in Costa Buena. What would happen if someone had found those letters?

And it wasn't like the Dawgs didn't know about her, anyway. They'd already kidnapped her once while he was in Maine. There was already a connection to him there.

If he cared for her, which he indeed did, then he should leave her alone. He should stay as far away from her as possible. He needed to be smarter if he wanted to protect her.

Abner Dewey pulled the truck to the side of the road. The new bridge loomed ahead.

"Thanks for the lift," Murray said.

The older man stuck out his right hand, and Murray shook it.

"Whatever you've got yourself into, son, I hope it all works out."

There was nothing more to say except, "Take care, Abner." As Murray slipped out of the truck, the older man said, "What about your money?"

Murray glanced back.

In Abner's fist was a wad of cash. "It's not exactly half of the insurance proceeds, but it's all I had available at the house. About four grand, but you earned it."

Murray smiled and took the money. "Thank you," he said.

Abner tapped his watch. "No, son. Thank you."

After he slipped out of the truck and into the rain, Murray slammed the door closed. The pickup revved once before driving away into the night. The guns in his jacket bounced against his hips as he approached the bridge.

"Murray," a voice said.

He spun and stuck a hand into his jacket.

Anna Herrick stood underneath an umbrella. In her freehand was a small brown paper bag. "You won't need that," she said and motioned toward his hand.

Murray released the gun he clutched inside his pocket and lifted his hand into the open.

"I wanted to see you off," she said, "and bring you this." She handed him the bag. "It's a sandwich and some snacks. To tide you over until you get someplace warm."

He clutched the bag to his chest. "Thank you."

"That girlfriend of yours. Is she for real?"

He nodded.

Anna glanced down. "Well, if anything changes with her, I'll be around Belfry for a while. You can give me a call."

Murray smiled but didn't want to offer any encouragement.

Anna tilted her umbrella back, stepped forward, and kissed Murray on the cheek. Without another word, she walked away, not bothering to look back.

It was his turn to move.

He hurried past the BRIDGE CLOSED signs and started across. Initially, he walked hurriedly, almost with abandon, as he didn't like the idea of being caught with nowhere to go. But when he realized there were large portions of the bridge missing, and that he could drop through to the water below, Murray slowed and began a careful, more methodical walk.

When he was halfway across, he felt more comfortable that no Dawgs awaited him now. He reached into a pocket, grabbed one of the guns, and threw it into the river. He never heard it plop into the raging water. Quickly, he repeated the process with the other weapon.

In several spots, he needed to shimmy across exposed steel beams carefully. One false step and he could fall into the rushing waters below. The falling rain made the girders slick, and more than once, he wobbled like he might lose his balance.

It felt like a lifetime getting across that bridge. Once Murray did, though, he stepped beyond another BRIDGE CLOSED sign and was on the mainland of Oregon again.

He breathed a sigh of relief.

Nearby, an engine started, and a pair of headlights flicked on.

Murray fought the desire to run. A Chevy Impala slowly pulled up next to him. When the passenger window rolled down, a plume of smoke escaped. He bent so he could see a gray-haired woman behind the wheel. She wore a flannel shirt and blue jeans. Tucked between her lips was a half-smoked cigarette.

The woman eyed him with scorn when she growled, "Get in."

"Who are you?" Murray asked.

"Your new witness inspector, Gayle Goodspeed."

She appeared too old and too frail to be an inspector. "Got proof?"

Goodspeed snatched the cigarette from her mouth. "The proof, Beauregard Smith," she said, "is that I drive away and leave you standing here long enough for those old pals of yours to realize you're off the island. After they grab you, you'll have all the proof you need. Is that good enough for you? Or do you want to continue to stand there like some slack-jawed fool?"

She tapped her cigarette into an empty soda can that sat in the middle console.

Murray straightened to glance up and down the highway. His life had gotten immensely complicated over the past several weeks. Marshal Onderdonk and Agent Ekleberry, as irritating as they were, offered him at least some comfort.

Goodspeed hollered at him from inside the car. "Make up your mind, little sister. I ain't got all day."

Little sister?

With a shake of his head, he yanked open the door and climbed into the car.

The marshal took a final drag on her cigarette before dropping it inside the soda can. It hissed out. The Chevy Impala lurched forward then, traveling eastbound.

"Where are we headed?" Murray asked.

Goodspeed spat out her window. "Illinois."

"Why there?" he asked.

"Seems you've gotten into some trouble on the coasts. The way I figure it, maybe you need to be in the heartland. Get around some people with some good, upstanding morals."

"And Illinois is it?"

She scrunched her nose and nodded. "It's my home state. You'll love the home of the Fighting Illini."

They rode in silence for a bit.

Finally, Murray asked, "Do I get a say in where I'm assigned?"

Goodspeed yanked the wheel and pulled to the side of the road. "You can get out of my car, little sister, or you can shut up. Make your choice."

Why did this woman already dislike him?

He never thought he would admit it, but he missed Marshal Ted Onderdonk.

When he didn't say anything, Gayle Goodspeed sniffed. "It figures. You're all talk, aren't you?"

"I was hoping for someplace a little warmer."

Goodspeed chuckled. "Don't cry, little sister. Where you're going, they've got all the amenities you could want."

He glanced at her. "Like what?"

The car lurched forward again, and Murray shook his head. What was it with marshals and their need to always tweak him? Did they get some sort of specialized training to mess with a guy's head?

It was going to be a long ride unless he made some attempt to make friends with her.

"So Illinois," Murray muttered.

"That's right. And in case you failed grade-school geography—" Goodspeed glanced at him. "It's the one squeezed between Iowa and Indiana."

Murray sniffed dismissively. "I know where Illinois is."

"Isn't that special? Now, sit back, shut up, and let me drive." Goodspeed reached for the radio. "Hope you like country music."

It was definitely going to be a long ride, Murray thought.

Beau Smith
returns in...

Cozy Up
to Trouble

ABOUT THE AUTHOR

Besides writing the Cozy Up Series, Colin Conway is the author of the 509 Crime Stories, a series of novels set in Eastern Washington with revolving lead characters. They are standalone tales and can be read in any order.

Colin is also the co-author of the Charlie-316 series. The first book in the series, *Charlie-316*, is a political/crime thriller and has been described as "riveting and compulsively readable," "the real deal," and "the ultimate ride-along."

He served in the U.S. Army and later was an officer of the Spokane Police Department. He has owned a laundromat, invested in a bar, and run a karate school. Besides writing crime fiction, he is a commercial real estate broker.

Colin lives with his beautiful girlfriend, three wonderful children, and a codependent Vizsla that rules their world.

Find out more at colinconway.com.